He looked down his long nose at her. "Be good enough not to interfere."

Mary Jane's bosom heaved, her nice eyes sparkled with temper. "Well, really it's not your business—"

He interrupted her. "Oh, but it is. I am here at your grandfather's request to attend to his affairs—at his urgent request, I should remind you before he should die—and here you are telling me what to do and what not to do. You're a tiresome girl."

With which parting shot, uttered in his perfect, faintly accented English, he went into the study.

Mary Jane, a gentle-natured girl for the most part, flounced into the sitting room, and quite beside herself with temper, poured herself a whiskey. It was unfortunate that Mr. Van Blocq chose to return, now, after five minutes.

"Good God, woman. Can't I turn my back for one minute without reaching for the whiskey bottle!"

She said carefully in a resentful voice, "You're enough to drive anyone to drink. Are you married? If you are, I'm very sorry for your wife."

He took her glass from her and set it down and poured himself a drink. "No, I'm not married," he said blandly, "so you may spare your sympathy."

Romance readers around the world will be sad to note the passing of **Betty Neels** this past June. Her career spanned thirty years and she continued to write into her ninetieth year. To her millions of fans, Betty epitomized romance, and yet she began writing almost by accident. She had retired from nursing, but her inquiring mind still sought stimulation. Her new career was born when she heard a lady in her local library bemoaning the lack of good romance novels. Betty's first book, *Sister Peters in Amsterdam,* was published in 1969, and she eventually completed 134 books. Her novels offer a reassuring warmth that was very much part of her own personality. She was a wonderful person as well as a hugely talented writer, and she will be greatly missed. Her spirit will live on in stories still to be published.

THE BEST *of*

BETTY NEELS

WINTER OF CHANGE

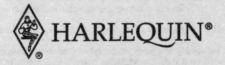

HARLEQUIN®

TORONTO • NEW YORK • LONDON
AMSTERDAM • PARIS • SYDNEY • HAMBURG
STOCKHOLM • ATHENS • TOKYO • MILAN • MADRID
PRAGUE • WARSAW • BUDAPEST • AUCKLAND

ISBN 0-373-51175-2

WINTER OF CHANGE

Copyright © 1973 by Betty Neels.

This edition published by arrangement with Harlequin Books S.A.

® and TM are trademarks of the publisher. Trademarks indicated with ® are registered in the United States Patent and Trademark Office, the Canadian Trade Marks Office and in other countries.

Visit us at www.eHarlequin.com

Printed in U.S.A.

CHAPTER ONE

SISTER THOMPSON made her slow impressive way down Women's Surgical, bidding her patients a majestic good morning as she went, her sharp eyes behind their glasses noticing every small defect in the perfection she demanded on her ward—and that applied not only to the nursing and care of the ladies lying on either side of her, but also to the exact position of the water jugs on the lockers, the correct disposal of dressing gowns, the perfection of the bedspreads and the symmetry of the pillows. The nurses who worked for her held her in hearty dislike, and when posted to her ward quickly learned the habit of melting away out of her sight whenever their duties permitted. Something which Mary Jane Pettigrew, her recently appointed staff nurse, was, at that particular time, quite unable to do. She watched her superior's slow, inevitable progress with a wary eye as she changed the dressing on Miss Blake's septic finger; she had no hope of getting it done before Sister Thompson arrived, for Miss Blake was old and shaky and couldn't keep her hand still for more than ten seconds at a time. Mary Jane, watching Nurse Wells and Nurse Simpson disappear, one into the sluice room, the other into the bathrooms at the end of the ward, wondered how long it would be before they were discovered—in the meantime, perhaps she could sweeten Sister Thompson's temper.

She fastened the dressing neatly and wished her superior a cheerful good morning which that good lady didn't bother to answer, instead she said in an arbitrary manner: 'Staff Nurse Pettigrew, you've been on this ward for two weeks and not only do you fail to maintain discipline amongst the nurses; you seem quite incapable of keeping the ward tidy. There are three pillows—and Miss Trump's top blanket, also Mrs Pratt's water jug is in the wrong place...'

Mary Jane tucked her scissors away in her pocket and picked up the dressing tray. She said with calm, 'Mrs Pratt can't reach it unless we put it on that side of her locker, Sister, and Miss Trump was cold, so I unfolded her blanket. May the nurses go to coffee?'

Sister Thompson cast her a look of dislike. 'Yes—and see that they're back before Mr Cripps' round.' She turned on her heel and went back up the ward and into her office, to appear five minutes later with the information that Mary Jane was to present herself to the Chief Nursing Officer at once, 'and,' added Sister Thompson, 'I suggest that you take your coffee break at the same time, otherwise you will be late for the round.'

Which meant that unless the interview was to be a split-second, monosyllabic affair, there would be no coffee. Mary Jane skimmed down the ward, making a beeline for the staff cloakroom. Whatever Sister Thompson might say, she was going to take a few minutes off in order to tidy her person. The room was small, nothing more than a glorified cupboard, and in order to see her face in the small mirror she was forced to rise on to her toes, for she was a small girl, only a little over five feet, with delicate bones and a tiny waist. She took one look at her reflection now, uttered a sigh and whipped off her cap so that she might smooth her honey-brown hair, fine and straight and worn in an old-fashioned bun on the top of her head. The face which looked back at her was pleasant but by no means pretty; only her eyes, soft and dark, were fine under their thin silky arched brows, but her nose was too short above a wide mouth and although her teeth were excellent they tended to be what she herself described as rabbity. She rearranged her cap to her satisfaction, pinned her apron tidily and started on her journey to the office.

Her way took her through a maze of corridors, dark passages and a variety of staircases, for Pope's Hospital was old, its ancient beginnings circumvented by more modern additions, necessitating a conglomeration of connecting passages. But Mary Jane, her thoughts busy, trod them unhesitatingly, having lived with them for more than three years. She had no idea why she was wanted, but while she was in the office it might be a good idea to mention that she wasn't happy on Women's Surgical. She had been aware, when she took the post, that it would be no bed of roses; Sister Thompson was notorious for her ill-temper and pernickety ways, but Mary Jane, recently State Registered, had felt capable of moving mountains... She would, she decided as she sped down a stone-flagged passage with no apparent ending, give in her notice at the end of the month and in the meantime start looking for another job. The thought of leaving Pope's was vaguely worrying, as she had come to regard it as her home, for indeed she had no home in the accepted sense. She had been an orphan from an early age, brought up, if one could call it that, by her grandfather, a retired Army colonel, who lived in a secluded house near Keswick and seldom left it. She had spent her holidays there all the while she was at the expensive boarding school to which he had sent her, and she had sensed his relief when she had told him, on leaving that admirable institution, that she wished to go to London and train to be a nurse, and in the three years or more in which she had been at Pope's she had gone to see him only once each year, not wishing to upset his way of living, knowing that even during the month of her visit he found her youthful company a little tiresome.

Not that he didn't love her in his own reserved, elderly fashion, just as she loved him, and would have loved him even more had he encouraged her to do so. As it was she accepted their relationship with good sense because she was a sensible girl, aware too that she would probably miss a good deal of the fun of life because she would need to work for the rest of it; even at the youthful age of twenty-two she had discovered that men, for the most part, liked good looks and failing that, a girl with a sound financial background, and she had neither, for although her grandfather lived comfortably enough, she had formed the opinion over the years that his possessions would go to some distant cousin she had never seen, who lived in Canada. True, old Colonel Pettigrew had educated her, and very well too, provided her with the right clothes and given her handsome presents at Christmas and on her birthday, but once she had started her training as a nurse, he had never once offered to help her financially—not that she needed it, for she had the good sense to keep within her salary and although she liked expensive clothes she bought them only when she saved enough to buy them. Her one extravagance was her little car, a present from her grandfather on her twenty-first birthday; it was a Mini and she loved it, and despite her fragile appearance, she drove it well.

The office door was firmly closed when she reached it and when she knocked she was bidden to enter at once the outer room, guarded by two office Sisters, immersed in paper work, one of whom paused long enough to wave Mary Jane to a chair before burying herself in the litter of papers on her desk. Mary Jane perched on the edge of a stool, watching her two companions, feeling sorry for them; they must have started out with a desire to nurse the sick, and look where they were now—stuck behind desks all day, separated from the patients by piles of statistics and forms, something she would avoid at all costs, she told herself, and was interrupted in her thoughts by the buzzer sounding its summons.

The Chief Nursing Officer was quite young, barely forty, with a twinkling pair of eyes, a nice-looking face and beautifully arranged hair under her muslin cap. She smiled at Mary Jane as she went in.

'Sit down, Staff Nurse,' she invited. 'There's something I have to tell you.'

'Oh lord, the sack!' thought Mary Jane. 'Old Thompson's been complaining...' She was deep in speculation as to what she had done wrong when she was recalled to her surroundings by her companion's pleasant voice.

'It concerns your grandfather, Nurse Pettigrew. His housekeeper telephoned a short time ago. He isn't very well and has asked for you to go to his home in order to look after him. Naturally you will wish to do so, although I've been asked to stress the fact that there's no'—she paused—'no cause for alarm, at least for the moment. I believe your grandfather is an old man?'

Mary Jane nodded. 'Eighty-two,' she said in her rather soft voice, 'but he's very tough. May I go at once, please?'

'As soon as you wish. I'll telephone Sister Thompson so that there's no need for you to go back to the ward. Perhaps when you get to your grandfather's, you'll let me know how things are.'

She was dismissed. She made her way rapidly to the Nurses' Home, thankful that she wouldn't have to face Sister Thompson, her mind already busy with the details of her journey. It was full autumn, it would be cold in Cumbria, so she would take warm clothes but as few as possible—she could pack a case in a few minutes. She was busy doing that when her bedroom door was flung open and her dearest friend, Janet Moore, came in. 'There's a rumour,' she began, 'someone overheard that you'd been sent to the Office.' Her eyes lighted on the little pile of clothes on the bed. 'Mary Jane, you've never been...no, of course not, you've never done anything really wicked in your life. What's up?'

Mary Jane told her as she squeezed the last sweater into her case, shut the lid and started to tear off her uniform. She was in slacks and a heavy woolly by the time she had finished, and without bothering to do more than smooth her hair, tied a bright scarf over it, pushed impatient feet into sensible shoes, caught up her handbag and the case and made for the door, begging her friend to see to her laundry for her as she went. 'See you,' she said briefly, and Janet called after her:

'You're not going now—this very minute? It's miles away—it'll be dark...'

'It's ten o'clock,' Mary Jane informed her as she made off down the corridor, 'and it's two hundred and ninety miles—besides, I know the way.'

It seemed to take a long time to get out of London, but once she was clear of the suburbs and had got on to the A1, she put a small, determined foot down on the accelerator, keeping the little car going at a steady fifty-five, and when the opportunity occurred, going a good deal faster than that.

Just south of Newark she stopped for coffee and a sandwich and then again when she turned off the A1 at Leeming to cross the Yorkshire fells to Kendal. The road was a lonely one, but she knew it well, and although the short autumn afternoon was already dimming around her, she welcomed its solitude after the rush and bustle of London. At Kendal she stopped briefly before taking the road which ran through Ambleside and on to Keswick. The day was closing in on her now, the mountains around blotting out the last of a watery sun, but she hardly noticed them. At any other time she would have stopped to admire the view, but now she scarcely noticed them, for her thoughts were wholly of her grandfather. The last few miles of the long journey seemed endless, and she heaved a sigh of relief as she wove the car through Keswick's narrow streets and out again on to the road climbing to Cockermouth. Keswick was quickly left behind; she was back in open country again and once she had gone through Thronthwaite she slowed the car. She was almost there, for now the road ran alongside the lake with the mountains crowding down to it on one side, tree-covered and dark, shutting out the last of the light, and there was only an odd cottage or two now and scattered along the faint gleam of the water, larger houses, well away from each other. The road curved away from the lake and then returned and there, between it and the water, was her grandfather's house.

It stood on a spit of land running out into the lake, its garden merging into the grass alongside the quiet water. It was of a comfortable size, built of grey stone and in a style much favoured at the beginning of the nineteenth century, its arched windows fitted with leaded panes, its wrought-iron work a little too elaborate and a turret or two ornamenting its many-gabled roof. All the same it presented a pleasing enough picture to Mary Jane as she turned the car carefully into the short drive and stopped outside the front porch. Its door stood open and the woman standing there came to meet her with obvious relief.

'Mrs Body, how lovely to see you! I came as quickly as I could—how's Grandfather?'

Mrs Body was pleasant and middle-aged and housekeeper to the old Colonel for the last twenty years or more. She took Mary Jane's hand and said kindly, 'There, Miss Mary Jane, if it isn't good to see you, I must say. Your grandfather's not too bad—a heart attack, as you know, but the doctor's coming this evening and he'll tell you all about it. But now come in and have tea, for you'll be famished, I'll be bound.'

She led the way indoors as she spoke, into the dim, roomy hall. 'You go up and see the Colonel, he's that anxious for you to get here—and I'll get the tea on the table.'

Mary Jane nodded and smiled and ran swiftly up the uncarpeted staircase, past the portraits of her ancestors and on to the landing, to tap on a door in its centre. The room she was bidden to enter was large and rather over-full of ponderous furniture, but cheerful enough by reason of the bright fire burning in the grate and the lamps on either side of the bed.

The Colonel lay propped up with pillows, an old man with a rugged face which, to Mary Jane's discerning eye, had become very thin. He said now in a thin thread of a voice, 'Hullo, child—how long did it take you this time?' and she smiled as she bent to kiss him; ever since he had given her the car, he had made the same joke about the time it took her to drive up from London. She told him now, her head a little on one side as she studied him. She loved him very much and he was an ill old man, but none of her thoughts showed on her calm, unremarkable features. She sat down close to the bed and talked for a little while in her pretty voice, then got up to go to her tea, telling him that she would be back later.

'Yes, my dear, do that. I daresay Morris will be here by then, he knows all about me.' He added wistfully, 'You'll stay, Mary Jane?'

She retraced her steps to his bed. 'Of course, Grandfather. I've no intention of going back until you're well again—I've got unlimited leave from Pope's,' she grinned engagingly at him, 'and you know how much I love being here in the autumn.'

Tea was a substantial meal; a huge plate of bacon and eggs, scones, home-made bread and a large cake, as well as a variety of jams and a dish of cream. Mary Jane, who was hungry, did justice to everything on the table while Mrs Body, convinced that she had been half starved in hospital, hovered round, urging her to make a good meal.

She did her best, asking questions while she ate, but Mrs Body's answers were vague, so it was with thankfulness that she went to meet the doctor when he rang the bell. She had known him since she was a little girl and held him in great affection, as he did her. He gave her an affectionate kiss now, saying, 'I knew you would come at once, my dear. You know your grandfather's very ill?'

They walked back to the sitting room and sat down. 'Yes,' said Mary Jane. 'I'll nurse him, of course.'

'Yes, child, I know you will, but that won't be for long. He'll rally for a few days, perhaps longer, but he's not going to recover. He was most anxious that you should come.'

'I'll stay as long as I can do anything to help, Uncle Bob—who's been looking after him?'

'Mrs Body and the district nurse, but he wanted you—there's something he wishes to talk to you about. I suggest you let him do that tomorrow morning when he's well rested.' He smiled at her. 'How's hospital?'

She told him briefly about Sister Thompson. 'It's not turning out quite as I expected, perhaps I'm not cut out to make a nurse...'

He patted her shoulder. 'Nonsense, there's nothing wrong with you, Mary Jane. I should start looking for another job and leave as soon as you can—at least...' He paused and she waited for him to finish, but he only sat there looking thoughtful and presently said: 'Well, I'll go and take a look—you'll be around when I come downstairs?'

He went away, and Mary Jane went along to the kitchen and spent some time helping Mrs Body and catching up on the local news until Doctor Morris reappeared. In the hall he said briefly: 'He's fighting a losing battle, I'm afraid,' then went on to give her his instructions, 'and I'll be in some time tomorrow morning,' he concluded.

There was a dressing room next to the Colonel's room. Mary Jane, who usually slept in one of the little rooms, moved her things into it, had a brief chat with her grandfather, settled him for the night and went down to the kitchen where the faithful Mrs Body was waiting with cocoa. They sat at the table, drinking it, with Major, the Colonel's middle-aged dog, sitting at their feet, and discussed the small problems confronting them. Mary Jane finished her cocoa and put down her cup. 'Well, now I'm here,' she said in her sensible way, 'you must have some time to yourself—these last few days must have been very tiring for you. If I'd known, I'd have come sooner.'

Mrs Body shook her head. 'Your grandfather wouldn't hear of it, not at first, but when Doctor Morris told him—he couldn't get you here fast enough,' she concluded, and sighed. 'All the same, I'll admit I'll be glad of an hour or so to myself. Lily comes up each morning as she always does, she's a good girl, and now you're here, I could get away for a bit.'

Mary Jane agreed. 'Supposing you take the Mini for a couple of hours each day? You could go to Keswick or Cockermouth if you want to do some shopping. I'll be quite all right here—I can go for a walk when you get back.'

The housekeeper gave her a grateful smile. 'That's kind of you, Miss Mary Jane, I'd like that. I want my hair done and one thing and another—you don't mind me using the Mini?'

'Heavens, no. Now I think I'll go to bed, it's been a long day. Will you be all right? I'll be in the dressing room and I've fixed Grandfather's bell and I shall leave the door open—besides, he's had a sedative. You will sleep? or shall I bring you something?'

'Bless you, child, I've never taken any of those nasty pills yet, and don't intend to. I'll sleep like a baby.'

It was a bright, clear morning when Mary Jane woke the next morning and her grandfather was still sleeping; he had wakened once in the small hours and she had gone and sat with him for an hour until he dozed off again; now he would probably sleep for another hour or more. She put on slacks and a sweater, tied her hair back and went downstairs. Mrs Body was already up, so they drank their early morning tea together and then Mary Jane took Major into the garden and across the grass to the lake's edge. The water was calm and as smooth as silk, the mountains reflected in it so that it took on their colour, grey and green. Across the lake Skiddaw loomed above the other peaks, the sun lending it a bronze covering for its granite slopes.

Mary Jane looked about her with pleasure as she threw sticks for Major, a pleasure tinged with sadness because the Colonel was ill, and although he was an old man, and didn't, she suspected, mind dying, she would miss him very much. He had been all the family she had known; now she would be alone, save for the cousin in Canada. She had never met him and her grandfather seldom mentioned him. She supposed that after her grandfather died, this cousin would inherit the house and whatever went with it. She knew nothing of the Colonel's affairs; he had encouraged her to earn her own living when she had left school and she had always imagined that he had done so because he couldn't afford to keep her idle at home, for although the house was a comfortable one and well furnished and there was no evidence of poverty, common sense told her that the old man and his housekeeper could live economically enough, whereas if she lived with them, she would need clothes and pocket money and holidays... She went back into the house, and after a reassuring peep at the Colonel, went to eat her breakfast.

Mrs Body left soon after Lily arrived and Mary Jane went upstairs to make her grandfather comfortable for the day. He seemed better, even demanding his razor so that he might shave himself, a request which she refused in no uncertain manner. Indeed, she fetched the old-fashioned cut-throat razor which he always used, and wielded it herself without a qualm, an action which caused him to ask her somewhat testily exactly what kind of work she did in hospital. There seemed no point in going too deeply into this; she fetched the post, opened his letters for him, and when he had read them, offered to read *The Times* to him. Perhaps it was her gentle voice, perhaps it was the splendid sports news, one or other of them sent him off into a sound sleep. She put the bell by his

hand and went downstairs. It was barely eleven
o'clock, Mrs Body wouldn't be back until the afternoon, Lily was bustling around the sitting room—
Mary Jane went into the garden, round to the front of
the house where she would be able to hear her grandfather's bell; there was a lot of weeding which needed
doing in the rose beds which bordered the drive.

She had been hard at it for fifteen minutes or so
when she became aware that a car had stopped before
the gate, and when she looked round she saw that it
was a very splendid car—a Rolls-Royce Corniche
convertible, the sober grey of its coachwork gleaming
against the green of the firs bordering the road behind
it. Its driver allowed the engine to idle silently while
he looked at Mary Jane, who, quite unable to recog-
nise the car or its occupant, advanced to the gate,
tossing back her mousey hair as she did so. 'Are you
lost?' she wanted to know. 'Cockermouth is only...'

'Thank you, but no, I am not lost,' said the man.
'This is Colonel Pettigrew's house.' It was, she realised, a statement, not an enquiry.

She planted her fork in between the roses, dusted
off her grubby hands and advanced a few steps. 'Yes,
it is.' She eyed him carefully; she had never seen him
before and indeed, she wouldn't have forgotten him
easily if she had, for he was a handsome man, not so
very young any more, but the grey hair at his temple
served to emphasise the intense blackness of the rest,
and his eyes were as dark as his hair, under thick
straight brows. His nose was a commanding one and

his mouth was firm above an angular jaw. Oh, most definitely a face to remember.

'I've come to see Colonel Pettigrew.' He didn't smile as he spoke, but looked her up and down in a casual uninterested fashion.

She ignored the look. 'Well, I'm not sure that you should,' she offered calmly. 'He's ill, and at the moment he's asleep. Doctor Morris will be here presently, and I think he should be asked first, but if you like to come in and wait—you'll have to be quiet.'

The eyebrows rose. 'My dear good young woman, you talk as though I were a pop group or a party of schoolchildren! I'm not noisy by nature and I don't take kindly to being told what I may and may not do.'

'Oh, pooh,' said Mary Jane, a little out of patience, 'don't be so touchy! Come in, do.' She added, 'Quietly.'

The car whispered past her and came to a silent halt at the door, and the man got out. There was a great deal of him; more than six foot, she guessed, and largely built too. She wondered who he was, and was on the point of asking when she heard the bell from her grandfather's room. 'There,' she shot at her companion, a little unfairly, 'you've woken him up,' and flew upstairs.

The Colonel looked refreshed after his nap. He said at once, 'I heard a car and voices. I'm expecting someone, but there's hardly been time...'

Mary Jane shook up a pillow and slipped it behind his head. 'It's a man,' she explained unhurriedly. 'He's got beetling eyebrows and he's got rather a super Rolls. He says he wants to see you, but I told him he couldn't until Uncle Bob comes.'

A faint smile lighted up her grandfather's face. 'Did you, now? And did he mind?'

'I didn't ask him.'

Her grandfather chuckled. 'Well, my dear, if it won't undermine your authority too much, I should like to see him—now. We have important business. Morris knows he's coming and I don't suppose he'll object. Tell him to come up.'

'All right, Grandfather, if you say so.'

She found the stranger in the sitting room, sitting in one of the comfortable old-fashioned chairs. He got to his feet as she went in and before she could speak, said: 'All right, I know my way,' and was gone, taking the stairs two at a time. She followed him into the hall just in time to hear the Colonel's door shut quietly on the old man's pleased voice. After a moment she went slowly into the garden again.

She was still there when Doctor Morris arrived, parked his elderly Rover beside the Rolls, greeted her cheerfully and added in a tone of satisfaction, 'Ah, good, so he's arrived—with your grandfather, I suppose?'

Mary Jane pulled a weed with deliberation. 'Yes, he is—and very high-handed, whoever he is, too. I asked him to wait until you came, but Grandfather heard us talking and wanted to see him at once—he said it was business. He seems better this morning, so I hope you don't mind?'

The doctor shook his head. 'No, I'm pleased.

You're both here now—your grandfather was worrying. I'll go up now.'

He left her standing there. She stared after him; he hadn't told her who the stranger was, but he obviously knew him. She went indoors, tidied herself and went along to get a tray of coffee ready, to find that Lily had already done so. 'And lunch, miss—I suppose the gentleman will be staying like last time. I'd better do some extra potatoes, hadn't I?'

Mary Jane agreed, desiring at the same time to question Lily about the probable guest, but if her grandfather had wanted to tell her, he could have done so, so too could Uncle Bob. If they wanted to have their little secrets, she told herself a trifle huffily, she for one didn't care. Probably the visitor was a junior partner to her grandfather's solicitor, but surely he wouldn't be able to afford a Rolls-Royce? She went outside again and had a good look at the car—it had a foreign number plate and it came from Holland, a clue which she immediately seized upon; the man was someone from her grandfather's oldest friend, Jonkheer van der Blocq, an elderly gentleman whom she had never met but about whom she knew quite a bit, for her grandfather had often mentioned him. Relieved that she had solved the mystery, she went back indoors in time to meet the doctor coming downstairs.

'There you are,' he remarked for all the world as though he had spent the last hour looking for her. 'Your grandfather wants you upstairs.' He eyed her thoughtfully. 'He's better, but you know what I mean by that, don't you? For the time being. Now run up, like a good girl. I'll be in the sitting room.'

She started up the stairs, remembering to call over her shoulder:

'There's coffee ready for you—would you ask Lily?' and sped on to tap on the Colonel's door and be bidden to enter.

The stranger was standing with his back to the window, his hands in his pockets, and the look he cast her was disconcerting in its speculation; there was faint amusement too and something else which she couldn't place. Mary Jane turned her attention to her elderly relative.

'Yes, Grandfather?' she asked, going up to the bed.

He eyed her lovingly and with some amusement on his tired old face.

'You're not a pretty girl,' he observed, and waited for her to answer.

'No, I know that as well as you—you didn't want me up here just to remind me, did you?' She grinned engagingly. 'I take after you,' she told him.

He smiled faintly. 'Come here, Fabian,' he commanded the man by the window.

And when he had stationed himself by the bed: 'Mary Jane, this is Fabian van der Blocq, the nephew of my old friend. He is to be your guardian after my death.'

Her eyes widened. 'My guardian? But I don't need a guardian, Grandfather! I'm twenty-two and I've never met Mr—Mr van der Blocq in my life before, and—and...'

'You're not sure if you like me?' His voice was bland, the smile he gave her mocking.

'Since you put the words into my mouth, I'm not sure that I do,' Mary Jane said composedly. 'And what do you have to be the guardian of?'

'This house will be yours, my dear,' explained her grandfather, 'and a considerable sum of money. You will be by no means penniless and there must be someone whom I can trust to keep an eye on you and manage your business affairs.'

'But I—' She paused and glanced across the bed to the elegant figure opposite her. 'Oh, you're a lawyer,' she declared. 'I wondered if you might be.'

Mr van der Blocq corrected her, still bland. 'You wondered wrongly. I'm a surgeon.'

She was bewildered. 'Are you? Then why...?' she went on vigorously, 'Anyway, Grandfather isn't going to die.'

The old gentleman in the bed made a derisive sound and Mr van der Blocq curled his lip. 'I am surprised that you, a nurse, should talk in such a fashion—you surely don't think that the Colonel wishes us to smother the truth in a froth of sickly sentiment?'

Mary Jane drew her delicate pale eyebrows together. 'You're horrible!' she told him in her gentle voice. It shook a little with the intensity of her feelings and she gave him the briefest of glances before turning back to her grandfather, whom she discovered to be laughing weakly.

'Don't you mind,' she demanded, 'the way this— this Mr van der Blocq talks?'

Her grandfather stopped laughing. 'Not in the least, my dear, and I daresay that when you know him better you won't mind either.'

She tossed her untidy head. 'That's highly unlikely. And now you're tired, Grandfather—you're going to have another nap before lunch.'

To her surprise he agreed quite meekly. 'But I want you back in the afternoon, Mary Jane—and Fabian.'

She agreed, ignoring the man staring at her while she rearranged blankets, shook up pillows and made her grandfather comfortable. This done to her satisfaction, she made for the door. Mr van der Blocq, beating her to it by a short head, opened it with an ironic little nod of his handsome head, and without looking at him she went through it and down the stairs to where Doctor Morris was waiting.

They drank their coffee in an atmosphere which was a little tense, and when the doctor got up to go, Mary Jane got up too, saying, 'I'll see you to your car, Uncle Bob,' and although he protested, did so. Out of their companion's hearing, however, she stopped.

'Look,' she said urgently, 'I don't understand— why is he to be my guardian? He doesn't even live in England, does he? and I don't know him—besides, guardians are old...'

The doctor's eyes twinkled. 'At a rough guess I should say he was nudging forty.'

'Yes? But he doesn't look...' She didn't finish the sentence. 'Well, it all seems very silly to me, and Grandfather...' She lifted her eyes to her companion.

'He's really not going to get any better? Not even if we do everything we possibly can?'

'No, my dear, and it will be quite soon now. I'll be back this evening. You know where to find me if you want me.'

She went back slowly to the sitting room and Mr Van der Blocq, lounging by the window, turned round to say: 'I don't suppose you got much help from Doctor Morris, did you?' He went on conversationally, 'If it is of any comfort to you, I dislike the idea of being your guardian just as much—probably more—than you dislike being my ward.'

Mary Jane sat down and poured more coffee for them both. 'Then don't. I mean, don't be my guardian, there's no need.'

'You heard your grandfather. You will be the owner of this house and sufficient money to make you an attractive target for any man who wants them.' He came across the room and sat down opposite her. 'I shall find my duties irksome, I dare say, but you can depend upon me not to shirk them.' He sat back comfortably. 'Do you mind if I smoke my pipe?'

She shook her head, and suddenly mindful of her duties as a hostess, asked, 'Where are you staying? Or are you perhaps only here for an hour or two?' She added hastily, 'You'll stay to lunch?'

A muscle twitched at the corner of his mouth. 'Thank you, I will—and I'm not staying anywhere,' his dark eyes twinkled. 'I believe the Colonel expected that I would stay here, but if it's too much trouble I can easily go to a hotel.'

'Oh no, not if Grandfather invited you. I'll go and see about lunch and get a room ready.' She got to her feet. 'There's sherry on the sofa table, please help yourself.'

Lily, she discovered when she got to the kitchen, had surpassed herself with Duchesse potatoes to eke out the cold chicken and salad, and there was a soup to start with; Mary Jane, feverishly opening tins to make a fruit salad, hoped that their guest wouldn't stay too long; she found him oddly disquieting and she wasn't even sure if she liked him, not that that would matter overmuch, for she supposed that she would see very little of him. She wasn't sure what the duties of a guardian were, but if he lived in Holland he was hardly likely to take them too seriously.

Ten minutes later, making up the bed in one of the guest rooms, she began to wonder for how long she was to have a guardian—surely not for the rest of her life? The idea of Mr van der Blocq poking his arrogant nose into her affairs, even from a distance, caused her to shudder strongly. She went downstairs, determined to find out all she could as soon as possible.

CHAPTER TWO

HER INTENTION MET with no success however. At lunch, her questions, put, she imagined, with suitable subtlety, were parried with a faint amusement which annoyed her very much, and when in desperation she tried the direct approach and asked him if, in the event of his becoming her guardian, it was to last a lifetime, he laughed and said with an infuriating calm:

'Now, why couldn't you have asked that in the first place? I have no intention of telling you, however. I imagine that your grandfather will explain everything to you presently.'

Mary Jane looked down her unassuming little nose. 'How long are you staying?' she asked with the icy politeness of an unwilling hostess. A question which met with an instant crack of laughter on the part of her companion. 'That depends entirely upon your grandfather's wishes, and—er—circumstances.'

She eyed him levelly across the table. 'You don't care tuppence, do you?' she declared fiercely. 'If Grandfather dies…'

She was unprepared for the way in which his face changed, and the quietness of his voice. 'Not if, when. And why pretend? Your grandfather knows that he is dying. He told me this morning that his one dread as he got older was that he would be stricken with some

lingering complaint which would compel him to lie
for months, dependent on other people. We should be
glad that he is getting his wish, as he is.' His eyes
swept over her. 'Go and do your face up, and look
cheerful, he expects us in a short while, and don't
waste time arguing that he must have another nap; I
happen to know that he won't be happy until he has
had the talk he has planned.'

Mary Jane got to her feet. 'You've no right to talk
to me like this,' she said crossly, 'and I have every
intention of tidying myself.'

She walked out of the room, and presently, having
re-done her face and brushed her hair until it shone,
she put it up as severely as possible, under the impression that it made her look a good deal older, and
went back downstairs, having first peeped in on the
Colonel, to find him dozing. So she cleared away the
lunch dishes and was very surprised when Mr van der
Blocq carried them out to the kitchen, and because
Lily had gone home, washed up, looking quite incon-
gruous standing at the sink in his beautifully cut suit.

The Colonel was awake when they went upstairs;
Mary Jane sat him up in his bed, arranging him comfortably with deft hands and no fuss while Mr van
der Blocq looked on, his hands in his pockets, whistling softly under his breath.

'And now,' said the Colonel with some of his old
authority, 'you will both listen to me, but first I must
thank you, Fabian, for coming at once without asking
a lot of silly questions—it must have caused you
some inconvenience, though I suppose you are now

of sufficient consequence in your profession to be able to do very much as you wish. Still, the journey is a considerable one—did you stop at all?'

His visitor smiled faintly. 'Once or twice, but I enjoy long journeys and the roads are quiet at night.'

Mary Jane cast him a surprised look. 'You've been travelling all night?' she wanted to know. 'You haven't slept?'

He gave her an impatient glance, his 'no' was nonchalant as he turned back to the old man in the bed. 'Enough that I'm here, I'm sure that Doctor Morris wouldn't wish us to waste your strength in idle chatter.' A remark which sent the colour flaming into Mary Jane's cheeks, for it had been so obviously directed against herself.

Her grandfather closed his eyes for a moment. 'You're quite right. Mary Jane, listen to me—this house and land will be yours when I die, and there is also a considerable amount of money which you will inherit—that surprises you, doesn't it? Well, my girl, your mother and father wouldn't have thanked me if I had reared a feather-brained useless creature, depending upon me for every penny. As it is, you've done very well for yourself, and as far as I'm concerned you can go on with your nursing if you've set your mind on it, though I would rather that you lived here and made it home,' he paused, a little short of breath, 'You're not a very worldly young woman, my dear, and I've decided that you should have a guardian to give you help if you should need it and see to your affairs, and cast an eye over any man who should want to marry you—you will not, in fact, be able to marry without Fabian's consent.' He paused again to look at her. 'You don't like that, do you? but there it is—until you're thirty.'

Mary Jane swallowed the feelings which could easily have choked her. She said, keeping her voice calm and avoiding Mr van der Blocq's eye, 'And your cousin in Canada, Grandfather? I always thought that he was—that he would come and live—I didn't know about the money.'

Her grandparent received this muddled speech with a frown and said with some asperity, 'Dead. His son's dead too, I believe—there was a grandson, I believe, but no one bothered to let me know. Besides, you love the place, don't you, Mary Jane?'

She swallowed the lump in her throat. If he was going to be coolly practical about his death, she would try her best to be the same.

'Yes, Grandfather, you know I do, but I don't need the money—I've my salary...'

'Have you any idea what a house like this costs in upkeep? Mrs Body, Lily, the rates, the lot—besides, you deserve to have some spending money after these last three years living on the pittance you earn.'

He closed his eyes and then opened them again, remembering something.

'You witness what I've said, Fabian? You understand your part in the business, eh? And you're still willing? I would have asked your uncle, but that's not possible any more, is it?'

Mr van der Blocq agreed tranquilly that he was

perfectly willing and that no, it was not possible for
his uncle to fulfil the duties of a guardian. 'And,' he
concluded, and his voice now held a ring of authority
and firmness, 'if you have said all you wished to say,
may I suggest that you have a rest? We shall remain
within call. Rest assured that your wishes shall be
carried out when the time comes.'

Mary Jane, without quite knowing how, found herself propelled gently from the room, but halfway
down the stairs she paused. 'It's so unnecessary!' she
cried. 'Surely I can run this house and look after my
own money—and it's miles for you to come,' she
gulped. 'And talking about it like this, it's beastly...'

He ignored that, merely saying coolly, 'I hardly
think you need to worry about my too frequent visits.'
He smiled a small, mocking smile and she felt
vaguely insulted so that she flushed and ran on down
the stairs and into the kitchen, where she found Mrs
Body, unpacking her shopping. She looked up as
Mary Jane rushed in and said: 'Hullo, Miss Mary
Jane, what's upset you? The Colonel isn't...?'

'He's about the same. It's that man—Mr van der
Blocq—we don't seem to get on very well.' She stood
in front of the housekeeper, looking rather unhappily
into her motherly face. 'Do you know him?'

'Lor', yes, my dear—he's been here twice in the
last few months, and a year or two ago he came with
that friend of your grandfather's, the nice old gentleman who lives in Holland—he's ill too, so I hear.'

Mary Jane waved this information on one side.
'He's staying,' she said. 'I don't know for how long.

I made up a bed in the other turret room. Ought we to do something about dinner?'

'Don't you worry about that, Miss Mary Jane—the Colonel told me that he'd be coming, so I've a nice meal planned. If you'll just set the table later on— but time enough for that. Supposing you go for a little walk just down to the lake and back. You'll hear me call easily enough and a breath of air will do you good before tea.'

Mary Jane made for the door and flung it open. She had a great deal to think about; it was a pity she had no one to confide in; she hadn't got used to the fact that her grandfather was dying, nor his matter-of-fact attitude towards that fact, and the strain of matching his manner with her own was being a little too much for her. She wandered down the garden, resolutely making herself think about the house and the future. She didn't care about the money, just as long as there was enough to keep everything going as her grandfather would wish it to be. She stopped to lean over a low stone wall, built long ago for some purpose or other but now in disuse. The Colonel, a keen gardener, had planted it with a variety of rock plants, but it had no colour now. She leaned her elbows on its uneven surface and gazed out to the lake and Skiddaw beyond, not seeing them very clearly for the tears which blurred her eyes. It was silly to cry; her grandfather disliked crying women, he had told her so on various occasions. She brushed her hand across her face and noted in a detached way that the mountains had a sprinkling of snow on their tops while the rest of them looked grey and misty and sad. She wished, like a child, that time might be turned back, that somehow or other today could have been avoided. Despite herself, her eyes filled with tears again; she wasn't a crying girl, but just for once she made no attempt to stop them.

Major had followed her out of the house, and sat close to her now, pressed against her knee, and when he gave a whispered bark she wiped her eyes hastily and turned round. Mr van der Blocq was close by, just standing there, looking away from her, across the lake. He spoke casually. 'You have had rather a shock, haven't you? You must be a little bewildered. May I venture to offer you a modicum of advice?' He went on without giving her a chance to speak. 'Don't worry about the future for the moment. It's not a bad idea, in circumstances such as these, to live from one day to the next and make the best of each one.'

He was standing beside her now, still not looking at her tear-stained face, and when she didn't reply he went on, still casually:

'Major hasn't had a walk, has he? Supposing we give him a run for a short while?'

Mary Jane, forgetful of the deplorable condition of her face, looked up at him. 'I don't like to go too far away…'

'Nor do I, but Mrs Body has promised to shout if she needs us—she's sitting with your grandfather now, and I imagine we could run fast enough if we needed to.' He smiled at her and just for a moment she felt warmed and comforted.

'All right,' she agreed reluctantly, 'if you say so,' and started off along the edge of the lake, Major at her heels, not bothering to see if Mr van der Blocq was following her.

They walked into the wind, not speaking much and then only about commonplace things, and as they turned to go back again Mary Jane had to admit to herself that she felt better—not, she hastened to remind herself, because of her companion but probably because she had needed the exercise and fresh air. She went straight to her grandfather's room when they got back to the house, but he was still sleeping, so obedient to Mrs Body's advice she went to the sitting room and had tea with her visitor. They spoke almost as seldom as they had done during their walk; indeed, she formed the opinion that her companion found her boring and hardly worthy of his attention, for although his manners were not to be faulted she had the strongest feeling that they were merely the outcome of courtesy; in other circumstances he would probably ignore her altogether. She sighed without knowing it and got up to feed Major.

When she got back to the sitting room, Mr van der Blocq got to his feet and with the excuse that he had telephone calls to make and letters to write, went away to the Colonel's study, which, he was careful to explain, his host had put at his disposal, leaving Mary Jane to wander out to the kitchen to help Mrs Body and presently to lay the table in the roomy, old-fashioned dining room before going up to peep once more at her sleeping grandfather before changing from her slacks and sweater into a grey wool dress she had fortuitously packed, aware as she did so of the murmur of voices from the Colonel's room.

She frowned at her reflection as she smoothed her hair into its neat bun and did her face. If Mr van der Blocq had wakened her grandfather in order to pester him with more papers, then she would have something to say to him! He came out of the adjoining room as she left her own, giving her a wordless nod and standing aside for her to go down the stairs. She waited until they were both in the hall before she said: 'I think you must be tiring Grandfather very much. I don't think he should be disturbed any more today— there's surely no need.'

He paused on his way to the study. 'My dear good girl, may I remind you that I am a qualified physician as well as a surgeon, and as such am aware of your grandfather's condition—better, I must remind you, than you yourself.' He looked down his long nose at her. 'Be good enough not to interfere.'

Mary Jane's bosom heaved, her nice eyes sparkled with temper. 'Well, really it's not your business…'

He interrupted her. 'Oh, but it is, unfortunately. I am here at your grandfather's request to attend to his affairs—at his urgent request, I should remind you, before he should die, and here you are telling me what to do and what not to do. You're a tiresome girl.'

With which parting shot, uttered in his perfect,

faintly accented English, he went into the study, closing the door very gently behind him.

Mary Jane, a gentle-natured girl for the most part, flounced into the sitting room, and quite beside herself with temper, poured herself a generous measure of whisky. It was a drink she detested, but now it represented an act of defiance, she tossed off a second glass too. It was unfortunate that Mr van der Blocq chose to return after five minutes, by which time the whisky's effects upon her hungry inside were at their highest; by then her head was feeling decidedly strange and her feet, when she walked to a chair, didn't quite touch the floor. It was unfortunate too that he saw this the moment he entered the room and observed coldly, 'Good God, woman, can't I turn my back for one minute without you reaching for the whisky bottle—you reek of it!' An exaggeration so gross that she instantly suspected that he had been spying upon her.

She said carefully in a resentful voice, 'You're enough to drive anyone to drink,' the whisky urging her to add, 'Are you married? If you are, I'm very sorry for your wife.'

He took her glass from her and set it down and poured himself a drink. 'No, I'm not married,' he said blandly, 'so you may spare your sympathy.' He sat down opposite her, crossed his long legs and asked, 'What did you do before you took up nursing? Were you ever here, living permanently?'

She cleared her fuzzy mind. 'No, I went to a boarding school, although I came here for the holidays, and then when I left school—when I was eighteen—I asked Grandfather if I might take up nursing and I went to Pope's. I've only been home once a year since then.'

'No boy-friends?' She hesitated and he added, 'I shall be your guardian, you know, I have to know a little about you.'

'Well, no.' Her head was clearer now. 'I never had much chance to meet any—only medical students, you know, and the housemen, and of course they always went for the pretty girls.' She spoke without self-pity and he offered no sympathy, nor did he utter some empty phrase about mythical good looks she knew she hadn't got, anyway. He said merely, 'Well, of course—I did myself, but one doesn't always marry them, you know.'

She agreed, adding in a matter-of-fact voice, 'Oh, I know that, I imagine young doctors usually marry where there's some money—unless they're brilliant with an assured future, and you can't blame them—how else are they to get on?'

'A sensible opinion with which I will not argue,' he assured her, his tone so dry that her slightly flushed face went slowly scarlet. It was fortunate that Mrs Body created a diversion at that moment by telling them that dinner would be ready in fifteen minutes and would Mary Jane like to take a quick peep at the Colonel first?

She was up in his room, pottering around because she sensed that he wanted company for a few minutes. When Doctor Morris arrived she waited while he examined his patient, adjusted his treatment, asked if he was through with his business, nodded his satisfaction at the answer and wished him a good night. Downstairs again, he accepted the drink offered him, muttered something to Mr van der Blocq and turned to Mary Jane.

'Your grandfather's happy; he's put his affairs in order, it's just a question of keeping him content and comfortable. You'll do that, I know, Mary Jane.' He stood up. 'I must be off, I've a couple more visits. Fabian, come to the car with me, will you?'

They talked very little over their meal and anything which they said had very little to do with the Colonel or what he had told them that day—indeed, Mr van der Blocq kept the conversation very much in his own hands, seeming not to notice her long silences and monosyllabic replies. She went to bed early, leaving him sitting by the fire, looking quite at home, with Major at his feet and still more papers on the table before him.

Once ready for bed, she went through to her grandfather's room, to find him awake, so she pulled up a chair to the dim lamp and made herself comfortable, declaring that she wasn't sleepy either. After a while he dozed off and so did she, to waken much later to find Mr van der Blocq standing looking down at her. She wasn't sure of the expression on his face, but what ever it was it changed to faint annoyance as she got silently to her feet. He said briefly, 'Go to bed,' and sat down in the chair she had vacated.

She was awakened by his hand on her shoulder.

She sat up at once with an urgent whispered 'Grandfather?' and when he nodded and handed her dressing gown from a chair, she jumped out of bed, thrust her arms into its sleeves anyhow and was half way to the door in her bare feet when he reminded her, 'Your slippers—it's cold.' Before she quite reached the door he caught her by the arm. 'Your grandfather wants to say something to you—don't try and stop him; he's quite conscious and as comfortable as he can be. I've sent for Morris.'

The Colonel was wide awake and she went straight to the bed and took his hand with a steady smile. He squeezed her fingers weakly.

'Plenty of guts—like me,' he whispered with satisfaction. 'Can't abide moaning women. Something I want you to do. Always wanted you to meet my friend—Fabian's uncle—he's ill too. Go and look after him—bad-tempered fellow, can't find a nurse who'll stay. Promised Fabian you'd go.' He looked at her. 'Promise?'

She said instantly, 'Yes, Grandfather, I promise. I'll look after him.'

'Won't be for long—Fabian will see to everything.'

She glanced across at the man standing on the other side of the bed, looking, despite pyjamas and dressing gown, as impassive and withdrawn as he always did. She wondered, very briefly, if he had any feelings at all; if so, they were buried deep. He returned her look with one of his own, unsmiling and thoughtful, and then went to the door. 'That's Morris's car—I'll let him in and wake Mrs Body.'

The Colonel died a couple of hours later, in his sleep, a satisfied little smile on his old face so that Mary Jane felt that to cry would be almost an insult— besides, had he not told her that she had guts? She did all the things she had to do with a white set face, drank the tea Mrs Body gave her, then had a bath and dressed to join Mr van der Blocq at the breakfast table, where she ate nothing at all but talked brightly about the weather. Afterwards, thinking about it, she had to admit that he had been a veritable tower of strength, organising a tearful Mrs Body and a still more tearful Lily, arranging everything without fuss and a minimum of discussion, telephoning the newspapers, old friends, the rector...

She came downstairs from making the beds just as he came out of the study and Mrs Body was coming from the kitchen with the coffee tray. He poured her a cup, told her to drink it in a no-nonsense voice, and when she had, marched her off for a walk, Major at their heels. It was a fine morning but cold, and Mary Jane, in her sweater and slacks and an old jacket snatched from the back porch, was aware that she looked plainer than even she thought possible—not that she cared. She walked unwillingly beside her companion, not speaking, but presently the soft air and the quiet peace of the countryside soothed her; she even began to feel grateful to him for arranging her day and making it as easy as he could for her. She felt impelled to tell him this, to be told in a brisk impersonal way that as her guardian it was his moral obligation to do so.

He went on: 'We need to talk; there is a good deal to be arranged. You will have to leave Pope's—you realised that already, I imagine. I think it may be best if I wrote to your Matron or whatever she is called nowadays, and explain your circumstances. Your grandfather's solicitor will come here to see you—and me, but there should be no difficulties there, as everything was left in good order. I think it may be best if you return to Holland with me on the day after the funeral; there's no point in glooming around the house on your own, and I can assure you that my uncle needs a nurse as soon as possible—his condition is rapidly worsening and extremely difficult.' He paused to throw a stone for Major. 'He was a good and clever man, and I am fond of him.'

Mary Jane stood still and looked at him. 'You've thought of everything,' she stated, and missed the gleam in his eyes. 'I only hope I'll be able to manage him and that he'll like me, because I promised Grandfather...'

Her voice petered out and although she gulped and sniffed she was quite unable to stop bursting into tears. She was hardly aware of Mr van der Blocq whisking her into his arms, only of the nice solid feel of his shoulder and his silent sympathy. Presently she raised a ruined face to his. 'So sorry,' she said politely. 'I don't cry as a general rule—I daresay I'm tired.'

'I daresay you are. We'll walk back now, and after lunch, which you will eat, you shall lie on the sofa in the study and have a nap while I finish off a few odd jobs.'

He let her go and strolled down to the water's edge while she wiped her eyes and blew her nose and re-tied her hair, and when they started back, he took her arm, talking, deliberately, of the Colonel.

Under his eye she ate her lunch, and still under it, tucked herself up in front of the study fire and fell instantly asleep. She awoke to the clatter of the tea tray as Mrs Body set it on the table beside the sofa and a moment later Doctor Morris came in.

The two men began at once to talk, and gradually, as she poured the tea and passed the cake, Mary Jane joined in. Before the doctor got up to go she realised with surprise that she had laughed several times. The surprise must have shown on her face, for Mr van der Blocq said with uncanny insight: 'That's better—your grandfather liked you to laugh, didn't he? Now, if you feel up to it, tell me how you stand at Pope's. A month's notice is normal, I suppose—have you any holidays due? Any commitments in London?'

'I've a week's holiday before Christmas, that's all, and I'm supposed to give a month's notice. There's nothing to keep me in London, but all my clothes and things are at Pope's.'

'We will pick them up as we go. What is the name of your matron?'

'Miss Shepherd—she's called the Principal Nursing Officer now.'

'Presumably in the name of progress, but what a pity. I shall telephone her now.' Which he did, with a masterly mixture of authority and charm. Mary Jane listened with interest to his exact explanations, which he delivered unembellished by sentiment and without any effort to enlist sympathy. It didn't surprise her in the least that within five minutes he had secured her resignation as from that moment.

When he had replaced the receiver, she remarked admiringly, 'My goodness, however did you manage it? I thought I would have to go back.'

'Manage what?' he asked coolly. 'I made a reasonable request and received a reasonable reply to it—I fail to see anything extraordinary in that.'

He returned to his writing, leaving her feeling snubbed, so that her manner towards him, which had begun to warm a little, cooled. It made her feel cold too, as though he had shut a door that had been ajar and left her outside. She went to the kitchen presently on some excuse or other, and sat talking to Mrs Body, who was glad of the company anyway.

'You've not had time to make any plans, Miss Mary Jane?' she hazarded.

'No, Mrs Body. You know that Grandfather left me this house, don't you? You will go on living here, won't you? I don't think I could bear it if you and Lily went away.'

The housekeeper gave her a warm smile. 'Bless you, my dear, of course we'll stay—it would break my heart to go after all these years, and Lily wouldn't go, I'm sure. But didn't I hear Doctor van der Blocq say that you would be going back to Holland with him?'

Mary Jane explained. 'It won't be for long, I imagine—if you wouldn't mind being here—do you suppose Lily would come and live in so that you've got company? I'm not sure about the money yet, but I'm sure there'll be enough to pay her. Shall I ask her?'

'A good idea, Miss Mary Jane. Supposing I mention it to her first, once everything's seen to? I must say the doctor gets things done—everything's going as smooth as silk and he thinks of everything. That reminds me, he told me to move your things back to your old room.

Mary Jane looked surprised. 'Oh, did he? How thoughtful of him,' and then because she was young and healthy even though she was sad: 'What's for dinner—I'm hungry.'

Mrs Body beamed. 'A nice bit of beef. For a foreign gentleman the doctor isn't finicky about his food, is he? and I always say there's nothing to beat a nice roast. There's baked apples and cream for afters.'

'I'll lay the table,' Mary Jane volunteered, and kept herself busy with that until Mr van der Blocq came out of the study, when she offered him a drink, prudently declining one herself before going upstairs to put on the grey dress once more. The sight of her face, puffy with tears and tense with her stored-up feelings, did little to reassure her, and when she joined Mr van der Blocq in the sitting room, the brief careless glance he accorded her deflated what little ego she had left. Sitting at table, watching him carving the beef with a nicety which augured well for his skill at his profession, she found herself wishing that he didn't regard her with such indifference—not, she told herself sensibly, that his opinion of her mattered one jot. He wasn't at all the sort of man she… He interrupted her thoughts.

'It seems to me a good idea if you were to call me Fabian. I do not like being addressed as Mr van der Blocq—inaccurately, as it happens. Even Mrs Body manages to address me, erroneously, as Doctor dear.' He smiled faintly as he looked at her, his eyebrows raised.

She studied his face. 'Well, if you want me to,' her voice was unenthusiastic, 'only I don't know you very well, and you're…'

'A great deal older than you? Indeed I am.'

It annoyed her that he didn't tell her how much older, but she went on, 'I was going to say that I find it a little difficult, because Grandfather told me that you were an important surgeon and I wouldn't dream of calling a consultant at Pope's by his first name.'

The preposterous idea made her smile, but he remained unamused, only saying in a bored fashion. 'Well, you are no longer a nurse at Pope's—you are Miss Pettigrew with a pleasant little property of your own and sufficient income with which to live in comfort.'

She served him a baked apple and passed the cream. 'What's a sufficient income?' she wanted to know.

He waved a careless, well kept hand, before telling her.

She had been on the point of sampling her own

apple, but now she laid down her spoon and said sharply, 'That's nonsense—that's a fortune!'

'Not in these days, it will be barely enough. There's your capital, of course, but I shall be in charge of that.' His tone implied that he was discussing something not worthy of his full attention, and this nettled her.

'You talk as though it were chicken feed!'

'That was not my intention. I'm sure you are a competent young woman and well able to enjoy life on such a sum. The solicitor will inform you as to the exact money.'

'Then why do I have to have you for a guardian?'

He put down his fork and said patiently, 'You heard your grandfather—I shall attend to any business to do with investments and so forth and have complete control of your capital. I shall of course see that your income is paid into your bank until you assume full control over your affairs when you are thirty. It will also be necessary for me to give my consent to your marriage should you wish to marry.'

She was bereft of words. 'Your consent—if I should choose' She almost choked. 'It's not true!'

'I am not in the habit of lying. It is perfectly true, set down in black and white by your grandfather, and I intend to carry out his wishes to the letter.'

'You mean that if anyone wants to marry me he'll have to ask you?'

He nodded his handsome head.

'But that's absurd! I never heard such nonsense…how could you possibly know—have any idea…?'

His voice had been cool, now it was downright cold. 'My dear good girl, let me assure you that I find my duties just as irksome as you find them unnecessary.'

This shook her. 'Oh, will you? I suppose they'll take up some of your time. I'll try not to bother you, then—I daresay there'll be no need for us to see much of each other.'

His lips twitched. 'Probably not, although I'm afraid that while you are at my uncle's house you will see me from time to time—he's too old to manage his own affairs, and my cousin, who lives with him, isn't allowed to do more than run the house.'

They were in the sitting room drinking their coffee when she ventured: 'Will you tell me a little about your uncle? I don't know where he lives or anything about him, and since I am to stay there…'

Mr van der Blocq frowned. 'Why should I object?' he wanted to know testily. 'But I must be brief; I'm expecting one or two telephone calls presently. He lives in Friesland, a small village called Midwoude. It is in fact on the border between Friesland and Groningen. The country is charming and there is a lake close by. The city of Groningen is only a few miles away; Leeuwarden is less than an hour by car. You may find it a little lonely, but I think not, for you are happy here, aren't you? My uncle, I have already told you, is difficult, but my cousin Emma will be only too glad to make a friend of you.'

'And you—you live somewhere else?'

'I live and work in Groningen.' He spoke pleasantly and with the quite obvious intention of saying nothing more. She had to be content with that, and shortly after that, when he went to answer his telephone call, Mary Jane went into the kitchen, helped Mrs Body around the place, laid the table for breakfast and went up to bed.

Now if I were a gorgeous creature with golden hair and long eyelashes, she mused as she wandered up the staircase, we might be spending the evening together—probably he had some flaxen-haired beauty waiting for him in Groningen. For lack of anything better to do and to keep her thoughts in a cheerful channel, she concocted a tale about Mr van der Blocq in which the blonde played a leading part, and he for once smiled frequently and never once addressed the creature as 'my dear good girl'.

The next few days passed quickly; there was a good deal to attend to and Major had to be taken for his walk, and time had to be spent with the Colonel's friends who called in unexpected numbers. The lawyer came too and spent long hours in the study with her guardian, although he had very little to say to her.

It wasn't until after the funeral, when the last of the neighbours and friends had gone, that old Mr North asked her to join him in the study and bring Mrs Body and Lily with her. Mary Jane half listened while he read the legacies which had been left to them both, it wasn't until they had gone and she was sitting by the fire with Fabian at the other end of the room that Mr North gave her the details of her own inheritance. The money seemed a vast sum to her; she had had no idea that her grandfather had had so much, even the income she was to receive seemed a lot of money. Mr North rambled on rather, talking about stocks and shares and securities and ended by saying:

'But you won't need to worry your head about this, Mary Jane, Mr van der Blocq will see to everything for you. I understand that you will be travelling to Holland tomorrow. That will make a nice change and you will return here ready to take your place in local society. I take it that Mrs Body will remain?'

She told him that yes, she would, and moreover Lily had agreed to live in as well, so that the problem of having someone to look after the house and Major was solved.

'You have no idea how long you will be away?' asked Mr North.

'None,' she glanced at Fabian, who took no notice at all, 'but I'm sure that Mrs Body will look after everything beautifully.'

The old gentleman nodded. 'And you? You will be sorry to leave your work at the hospital, I expect.'

She remembered Sister Thompson. 'Yes, though I was thinking of changing to another hospital.' She smiled at him. 'Now I shan't need to.'

He went shortly afterwards and she spent the rest of the day packing what clothes she had with her and making final arrangements with Mrs Body before taking Major for a walk by the lake. It was a clear evening with the moon shining. Mary Jane shivered a little despite her coat, not so much with cold as the knowledge that she would miss the peace and quiet even though she had it to come back to.

She went indoors presently and into the study to wish Fabian good night. He stood by her grandfather's desk while she made a few remarks about their journey and then said a little shyly, 'You've been very kind and—and efficient. I don't know what we should have done without your help. I'm very grateful.'

He rustled the papers in his hand and thanked her stiffly, and she went to her room, wondering if he would ever unbend, or was he going to remain coldly polite and a little scornful of her for the rest of their relationship? Eight years, she told herself as she got into bed, seemed a long time. She would be thirty and quite old, and Fabian would be…she started to guess and fell asleep, still guessing.

CHAPTER THREE

MARY JANE HAD never travelled in a Rolls-Royce—she found it quite an experience. Fabian was a good driver and although he spoke seldom he was quite relaxed, she sat silently beside him, thinking about the last two weeks—such a lot had happened and there had been so much to plan and arrange; she hoped she had forgotten nothing—not that it would matter very much, for her companion would not have overlooked the smallest detail. He had told her very little about the journey, beyond asking her to be ready to start at eight o'clock in the morning.

They were on the motorway now, doing a steady seventy, and would be in London by early afternoon, giving her ample time in which to pack her things at the hospital before they left for the midnight ferry.

'Anything you haven't time to see to you can leave,' he had told her, 'and arrange to send on the things you don't want—Mrs Body can sort them out later. You can buy all you need when we get to Holland.'

'Oh no, I can't, I've only a few pounds.'

'I will advance you any reasonable sum—do you need any money now?'

'No, thank you, but what about my fare?'

'Mr North and I will take care of such details.'

They had settled into silence after that. Mary Jane
stared through the window as the Rolls crept up behind each car in turn and passed it. Presently she
closed her eyes against the boredom of the road, the
better to think. But her thoughts were muddled and
hazy; she hadn't slept very well the night before, and
fought a desire to doze off, induced by the extreme
comfort of the car, and had just succeeded in reducing
her mind to tolerable clarity when her efforts were
shattered by her companion's laconic, 'We'll stop for
coffee.'

She glanced at her watch; they had been on the
road for just two hours and Stafford wasn't far away.
'That would be nice,' she agreed pleasantly, and was
a little surprised when he left the motorway, taking
the car unhurriedly down side roads which led at last
to a small village.

'Stableford,' read Mary Jane from the signpost.
'Why do we come here?'

'To get away from the motorway for half an hour.
There's a place called The Cocks—ah, there it is.' He
pulled up as he spoke.

The coffee was excellent and hot, and Mary Jane
ate a bun because breakfast seemed a long time ago,
indeed, a meal in another life.

'What time shall we get to London?' she wanted
to know.

'A couple of hours, I suppose. We will have a late
lunch before I take you to Pope's. I'll call for you
there at seven o'clock.'

'The boat doesn't go until midnight, does it?'

'We shall dine on the way.'

'Oh.' She felt somehow deflated; if he had said something nice about dining together, or even asked her—obviously he was performing a courteous duty with due regard to her comfort and absolutely no pleasure on his part. She followed him meekly out to the car and for the remainder of the journey only spoke when she was spoken to and that not very often. Only when they were driving through London's northern suburbs did he remark: 'We'll go to Carrier's, it's an easy run to Pope's from there.'

The restaurant was down a passage, double-fronted and modern, and Mary Jane, by now famished, chose fillet of beef in shirtsleeves, because it sounded quaint and filling at the same time. She was given a dry sherry to drink before they ate; she would have preferred a sweet one, but somehow Fabian looked the kind of man who would wish to order the drinks himself and she felt certain that he knew a great deal more about them than she ever would; she might be a splendid nurse, a tolerable cook and handy in the garden, but the more sophisticated talents had so far eluded her. It surprised her when he suggested, after she had disposed of the beef in its shirtsleeves and he had eaten his carpet bag steak, that she might like to sample Robert's Chocolate Fancy.

'Women like sweet things,' he told her tolerantly, and asked for the cheese board for himself.

Pope's looked greyer, more old-fashioned and more hedged in by the towering blocks of flats around it than ever before. 'You'll have to see the Matron—

you had better do that first,' said Fabian as he helped her out of the car. 'Do you want me to come with you?'

She declined politely and with secret regret; it would have been a pleasure to have walked through the hospital with Fabian beside her; she could just imagine the curious and envious glances that would have been cast at her.

He nodded. 'Good. I've one or two things to do. I'll be here at seven exactly.'

There was a great deal for her to do too. After the interview with Miss Shepherd, which was unexpectedly pleasant, there was a brief visit to Women's Surgical, where Sister Thompson wasn't pleasant at all, and then a long session of packing in her room. It was amazing what she had collected over the years! After due thought she packed a trunk with everything she judged might be unsuitable in a Dutch winter, which left her with some thick tweeds in a pleasing shade of brown, a variety of sweaters, a couple of jersey dresses and a rather nice evening dress she couldn't resist taking, although she saw no chance of wearing it. It was pale blue and green organza with long tight sleeves and a pie-frill collar, and it suited her admirably.

When she had finished packing she went along to the sitting room, where most of her friends were having tea, and found so much to talk about that she had to hurry to complete the tiresome chores of handing in her uniform to the linen room and waiting while it was checked, and then running all over the home to hand in the key of her room, both tasks requiring patience while the appropriate persons were found, the right forms filled in and signed and the farewells made, but she was at the hospital entrance by seven o'clock, wearing the brown tweeds and a felt hat which did nothing for her at all. All the same, she looked nice; her handbag and gloves and shoes were good and the tweed suit and coat suited her small slender person.

She reached the door just as Fabian drew up and got out of the car. He gave her a laconic 'Hullo', put her case in the boot and enquired about the rest of the luggage.

'It's in my trunk—one of my friends will send it on to Mrs Body.'

'Good. And Miss Shepherd—any difficulties?'

'No, thank you. None.'

'Get in, then.'

She didn't much like being ordered about, she was on the point of saying so when those of her closer friends who were off duty or who had been able to escape from their wards for a few minutes arrived in a chattering bunch to see her off. They embraced her in turn and with some warmth, at the same time taking a good look at Mr van der Blocq, who bore their scrutiny with a faint smile and complete equanimity, even when Penny Martin, the prettiest and giddiest of the lot of them, darted forward and caught him by the arm.

'Take care of Mary Jane,' she begged him with the faint lisp which most of the housemen found irresistible, 'and if you want another nurse at any time, I'd love to come.'

He smiled down at her, and Mary Jane, glimpsing the charm of it, felt quite shaken by some feeling she had no time to consider. He had never smiled at her like that; he must dislike her very much. The supposition caused her to be very quiet as they drove away from the cheerful little group on the steps, in fact, she didn't speak at all until they had crossed the river, gone through Southwark and joined the A2.

'You'll miss your friends,' commented her companion, slowing down for the traffic lights, 'and hospital life.' The car swept ahead again. 'There's no reason why you shouldn't go back to work there later on—you could spend your holidays in Cumbria.'

'Oh, I wouldn't do that,' declared Mary Jane, startled out of her silence. 'I shall like living in Grandfather's house and I shall find plenty to do. I shall miss Pope's, of course, but not the ward I was on.'

He shot her a brief, amused glance. 'Oh? Tell me about it.'

She did, rather haltingly at first, but he seemed interested and she found herself saying more than she intended.

'There is certainly no point in you going back to Women's Surgical,' he agreed. 'It sounds a joyless place, and your Sister Thompson needs to go on the retirement list.'

'But she's quite young, only forty.'

'You think that forty is quite young?'

'Heavens, yes.' She broke off as he turned the car

down a side road. 'Where are we going? I thought
this led to the M2.'

'There's a good place at Hollingbourne, and we
have plenty of time.'

The restaurant was pleasantly quiet and the food
exceptional. Mary Jane was beginning to think that
Fabian wouldn't go anywhere unless the food and the
service were near perfection. She remembered the
simple meals she and Mrs Body had cooked and wondered, as she ate her Kentish roast duckling, if he had
enjoyed them. Probably not.

They kept up a desultory conversation as they ate—
the kind of conversation, she told herself hopelessly,
that one sustained with fellow patients in a dentist's
waiting room. Before she could stop the words, they
popped out of her mouth. 'What a pity we don't get
on.'

If she had hoped to take him by surprise, she had
failed. His expression didn't change as he answered
in the pleasantest of voices.

'Yes, it is. Probably as we get to know each other
better, our—er—incompatibility will lessen.' He
smiled briefly and changed the subject abruptly. 'Tell
me, do you ride? If so, there is a good stables near
my uncle's house—they could let you have a mount.'

'Oh, could they? I should like that. I'm not awfully
good, but I enjoy it.'

'In that case you had better not go out alone.'

Which remark compelled her to say, 'Oh, I can ride
well enough, you needn't worry about that—it's just
that I'm not a first-class horsewoman.'

They sipped coffee in silence until she said defiantly, 'I shall buy a horse when I get back home,'
and waited to see what he would say. She was disappointed when he replied blandly, 'Why not? Shall
we go?'

They were at Dover with time to spare. They left
the car in the small queue and had coffee in the restaurant and Fabian bought her an armful of magazines. Once on board he suggested that she should go
to her cabin. 'We berth very early,' he warned her,
'half past four or thereabouts. We'll stop for breakfast
on the way to Friesland.'

His advice was sound. Mary Jane slept for a few
hours, and fortified by tea, joined him on deck as the
boat docked, and then followed him down to the car
deck. There was no delay at all as they landed; they
were away in a few minutes, tearing down the cob-
bled street towards the Dutch border.

The Rolls bored through the motorway from An-
twerp towards the frontier and Breda, going through
the town without stopping. It was quiet and dark, although a slow dawn was beginning to lighten the sky;
by the time they reached Utrecht there was a dim,
chilly daylight struggling through the clouds. Mary
Jane shivered in the warm car and Fabian spoke after
miles of silence. 'We'll stop here and have breakfast.'

It seemed a little early for there to be anywhere
open, but he stopped the car outside Smits Hotel, said,
'Stay where you are,' and went inside to return very
quickly and invite her inside, where she was welcomed by the hall porter with a courtesy she would

have found pleasant in broad daylight, let alone at that early hour of the morning, but Fabian seemed to take it all very much for granted, as he did the breakfast which was presently set before them. They ate at leisure, lingering over a final cup of coffee while he explained the route they were to follow. 'Less than a hundred miles,' he told her. 'We shall be at my uncle's house for coffee.'

And they were, after a drive during which Mary Jane, after several efforts at polite conversation, had become progressively more and more silent, staring out at the flat, frost-covered fields on either side of the road, observing with interest the cows in their coats, the large churches and the small villages so unlike her own home, and wishing with all her heart that she was back there—she even wished she was back at Pope's, coping with Sister Thompson's petty tyranny, but when her companion said, 'Only a few more miles now,' she pulled herself together; self-pity got one nowhere, and if Grandfather could know what she was thinking now he would be heartily ashamed of her show—even to herself—of weakness.

She sat up straight, rammed the unbecoming hat firmly upon her head and said, 'I'm glad, and I'm sure you must be too—travelling with someone you dislike can be very tiresome.'

Mr van der Blocq allowed a short sharp exclamation to leave his lips. 'Does that remark refer to myself or to you?' he queried silkily.

'Both of us.' She spoke without heat and lapsed into silence, a silence she would have liked to break

as he took the car gently through a very small village—cluster of one-storied cottages, a shop and an
over-sized church—and turned off the road through
massive iron gates and a tree-lined drive, and pulled
up before his uncle's house. She would have liked to
exclaim over it, for it was worthy of comment; built
of rose brick with a steep slate roof and an iron bal-
cony above its massive front door. It had two stories,
their windows exactly matching, and all with shutters.
It reminded her of some fairy tale, standing there silent, within the semicircle of sheltering trees, most of
them bare now. She was impressed and longed to say
so.

Fabian got out, came round to help her out too and
walked beside her up the shallow steps to the opening
door. A white-haired man stood there, neatly dressed
in a dark suit and looking so pleased to see them that
she deduced, quite rightly, that this wasn't Jonkheer
van der Blocq. Fabian quickly put her right, explaining as he shook the old man's hand, 'This is Jaap, he
has been in the family for forty years—he sees to
everything and will be of great help to you.'

Mary Jane put out a hand and had it gently wrung
while Jaap made her welcome—presumably—in his
own language. She nodded and smiled and followed
him into a handsome lobby and through its inner glass
doors to the hall, an imposing place, its walls hung
with dark, gilt-framed portraits, vicious-looking
weapons and a variety of coats of arms. It needed
flowers, she decided as she glanced about her, something vivid to offset the noble plastered ceiling and

marble floor with its dim Persian rugs. She was arranging them in her mind's eye when Fabian said: 'The sitting room, I suppose—the first door on the left.'

She followed Jaap through a double door into a room whose proportions rivalled those of the hall—the ceiling was high, the walls, painted white and ornamented at their corners with a good deal of carved fruit and flowers, carried a further selection of paintings. The furniture was massive and she had the feeling that excepting for the easy chairs flanking the large open fire, and the Chesterfield drawn up before it, the seating accommodation would be uncomfortable—an opinion which Fabian probably shared, for he advised her to take a chair by the fire, taking her coat and tossing it to Jaap.

'My cousin will be here in a moment,' he told her, and went to look out of the windows, while Mary Jane, left to herself, rearranged the furniture in her mind, set a few floral arrangements on the various tables and regarded with awe a large cabinet on the opposite wall; it was inlaid, with a good deal of strapwork, and she considered it hideous.

'German?' she asked herself aloud.

'You're right,' agreed Fabian from the window. 'The Thirty Years' War or thereabouts, I believe, and frankly appalling.'

She turned to look at him. 'Now isn't that nice, we actually agree about something!' She added hastily, 'I don't mean to be rude—I have no business to pass an opinion...'

He shrugged his wide shoulders. 'I'm flattered that we should share even an opinion.'

'Now that's a...' She was saved from finishing the forceful remark she was about to make by the entry of a lady into the room. The cousin, without doubt—fortyish, tall and thin and good-looking, her face marred by the anxious frown between her brows and the look of harassment she wore. Indeed, she appeared to be so hunted that Mary Jane expected to see her followed by Fabian's uncle in one of his more difficult moods. But no one else appeared; the lady trod across the room to Fabian, crying his name in a melodramatic fashion, and flung her arms around him. He received her embrace with a good-humoured tolerance, patted her on the shoulder and said in English: 'Now, Emma, you can stop behaving like a wet hen. Here is Mary Jane come to nurse Oom Georgius.'

He turned round and went to Mary Jane's side. 'This is my cousin Emma van der Blocq—I'm sure you will be good friends, and I know she is delighted to have you here to lighten her burden.'

'Indeed yes,' his cousin joined in, shaking Mary Jane's hand in an agitated way. 'I'm quite worn out, for my father thinks I am a very poor nurse and I daresay I am—I'm sure you will be able to manage him far better than I.' She sighed deeply. 'The nurses never stay.'

It sounded as though the old gentleman was going to be a handful, Mary Jane thought gloomily, but she had promised her grandfather, and in a way she was glad, because she would be too occupied to brood over his death. She said in her pleasant voice, 'I'll do my best. Perhaps when you have the time, you will tell me what you would like me to do.'

Cousin Emma became more agitated than ever. 'Oh yes, of course, but first you shall see your room and we will have lunch.' She looked at Fabian. 'You will go and see Father?'

He nodded and followed them out of the room and up the elegant staircase at one side of the hall, but on the landing they parted, he going to the front of the house while Mary Jane and her hostess entered a room at the head of the stairs. It was a large room, but not, she was relieved to see, nearly as large as the sitting room. It was furnished with a quantity of heavy Mid-Victorian furniture, all very ornate, carved and inlaid. The bed was a ponderous affair too, but the curtains and coverlet were pretty and the carpet was richly thick under her feet.

Here she was left alone to tidy herself before going downstairs again, something she was about to do when she was halted by a thunderous voice from behind a pair of handsome doors across the landing, bellowing something in Dutch, and a moment later Fabian appeared, to lean over the balustrade as she went down the stairs and ask if she would be good enough to visit his uncle.

The room they entered was vast, with a fourposter bed dwarfed against one wall and a great many chests and tallboys and massive cupboards. In the centre of this splendour sat Jonkheer van der Blocq, facing a roaring fire. And a handsome old man he was too, with white hair, a little thin on top, and Fabian's features. He didn't wait for his nephew to speak but began at once in a stentorian voice.

'Hah—so my good old friend died, and you are the Mary Jane he wrote so much of.' He produced a pair of spectacles and planted them upon his nose and stared at her. 'A dab of a girl, too. He promised me that if I should outlive him, he would send you to me. Nurses,' he went on in a triumphant voice, 'don't stay. Do you suppose you will?'

Mary Jane walked up to his chair, not in the least put out. 'I don't see why not,' she said in a reasonable voice, 'and anyway, I promised Grandfather I would. I'm not easily upset, you know.' She gave him a kind smile and he croaked with laughter. 'We'll see about that! At any rate you will be a change from that fool daughter of mine, always fussing around.'

'I daresay she wants to help you, but some people—and you, I suspect, aren't easy to do things for; they find fault all the time.'

He sat back against his cushions and she thought that he might explode; instead he burst out laughing. 'Dammit, if you're not like your grandfather!' he declared. 'No looks but plenty of spirit. I shall come down to lunch.' He turned to Fabian. 'And you, what do you think of her, eh?'

'I have no doubt that Mary Jane is an excellent nurse.'

'That wasn't what I meant. However, you may give me an arm and we'll go down. I rather fancy a glass of *Genever* before we lunch.'

'You'll not get it,' observed his nephew good-humouredly. 'A glass of white wine is all that Trouw allows you, and that's what you will have.'

The old man, far from being annoyed at this arbitrary remark, chuckled, and the three of them went down to the dining room in the friendliest possible way. The old gentleman's good humour lasted throughout the meal, and when Fabian got up to go, saying that he had an appointment that afternoon in Groningen, begged him to come again as soon as he could. 'Though I daresay you have a good deal of work to catch up on. How long have you been away?'

And when Fabian told him he continued: 'It will take you a week or two to work everything off, I daresay. Well, come when you can, Fabian.'

His thunderous voice sounded wistful and Mary Jane guessed that he was fond of his nephew, though probably nothing on earth would make him admit to it. Bidden by her host to see Fabian into his car, she walked a little self-consciously to the door and stood in the lobby while he spoke to Jaap, but presently he turned to her and said:

'Doctor Trouw will be here this evening, I believe. He speaks English and will explain all there is to know about my uncle. I hope it has been made clear to you that you are a guest here as well as a nurse, although you will doubtless find yourself called upon frequently enough if my uncle becomes particularly difficult.'

She raised surprised eyes to his. 'A guest? But I understood Grandfather to say that I was to take care of your uncle, I know he's not in bed, but he needs someone, and he's a lot more ill than he allows, isn't he? And he said himself that nurses don't stay. Does he really dislike your cousin looking after him?'

He gave a short laugh. 'I assure you that he does, nor does she like looking after him. Do as you think fit, but I for one shall not hold you to your promise, for you had no idea what it might entail when you gave it, and nor, I believe, did your grandfather. Uncle Georgius is going to get worse very soon now, and he will be what you so aptly describe in your language as a handful.'

'Look,' said Mary Jane patiently, 'you came over to Grandfather when he sent for you and it must have been inconvenient, but I don't think you would have refused, would you? Well, neither shall I.'

She gave him a determined little nod and the corner of his mouth twitched a little. 'Very well,' he said blandly, and turned to go.

'Just a minute,' she was self-conscious again, 'I want to thank you for making my journey so comfortable and for doing so much for us.' She looked at him earnestly. 'You didn't know any of us well, you could so easily have refused—you had every right. I—I heard what your uncle said about your backlog of patients.'

'Like you, I keep my word,' he told her. 'Goodbye.'

She watched the Rolls slip away between the trees and told herself that she was well rid of such a cold, disagreeable man, and the feeling which she ascribed to relief at his going was so strong that she very nearly burst into tears.

Mary Jane slipped into the life of the big, silent house quite easily. She was an adaptable girl and her training had made her more so. In only a few days she had taken over all the tiresome chores which Emma van der Blocq disliked so much; the persuading of the old gentleman to rise in the morning when he flatly refused, the coaxing of him to go to bed at a reasonable hour—more, the battle of wills which was fought daily over the vexed question as to whether his pills were to be taken or not. But at least he slept well once he was in his bed and she had turned out the lights save for one small lamp, turned his radio to a thread of sound, arranged the variety of odds and ends he insisted upon having on his bedside table and wished him a cheerful goodnight, however grumpy he was. She was free then, but too tired to do anything other than write an odd letter or so or leaf through a magazine. She was free during the day too, as she was frequently told, both by Jonkheer van der Blocq and his daughter, but somehow it was difficult to get away, for if the old gentleman didn't want her, Emma van der Blocq did, even if only for a gossip. It wasn't until several days after her arrival that Mary Jane, during the course of one of these chats, asked her hostess why Jaap always referred to her as Freule—a question which kept Emma van der Blocq happy for an entire afternoon, explaining the intricacies of the Dutch nobility. She added a wealth of information regarding their titles, their houses and lands to a fascinated Mary Jane, who at the end of this dissertation, asked, 'So what do I call Fabian? He's a surgeon—is he Mister or Doctor?'

Cousin Emma looked slightly taken aback. 'But of course you have not fully understood. He is also Jonkheer, he is also a professor of surgery, you comprehend? Therefore he is addressed as Professor Jonkheer van der Blocq.'

'My goodness,' observed Mary Jane, 'what a mouthful!' Now she knew why he had looked so amused when she had addressed him as Mister. It had been nice of him not to say anything, though it surprised her that he hadn't taken the opportunity of discomfiting her. Her companion went on earnestly, 'I am old-fashioned enough to set great store upon these things, but I believe that the young people do not. Fabian may not be young any more, but he does not care in the least about his position, he...' She was interrupted by the entry of Corrie, the maid, begging her to ask Miss to go at once to the master of the house, and as Mary Jane got obediently to her feet, she said: 'What a blessing you are to us all. You do not know the relief I feel at not having to answer every call from Papa's room.'

And Mary Jane, skipping up the stairs for the tenth time that day, could well believe her. She was a little puzzled that nobody had offered to relieve her of her duties from time to time—it would be all right for a week or so, but she began to feel the need for a little relaxation and exercise and for some other distraction

other than card games and Cousin Emma's rather the-
atrical conversation.

It was the next afternoon, when after a fruitless
effort on her part to escape for a walk, she was playing cards with her patient, that he wanted to know
what she thought of Fabian.

'I don't know him well enough to form an opinion,'
she told him in a matter-of-fact way. 'He saw to every
thing very nicely—we couldn't have managed without him, and Grandfather liked him.' She paused and
searched her memory. 'Everyone liked him,' she said
in surprise.

'But not you?'

Until that moment she hadn't realised that she had
never analysed her feelings towards Fabian. 'I've not
thought about it.'

The old gentleman persisted, 'Perhaps he doesn't
like you?'

She shuffled the cards and dealt them. 'Probably
not. One gets on better with some people than others.'

'You're not much to look at.'

'No—it's your turn.'

He slammed down a card. 'Men fall for a pretty
face.'

'So I should imagine.' She smiled at him across the
card table and he glowered back.

Presently he went on, 'A pretty face isn't everything. You're delightful company, Mary Jane; it was
good of your grandfather to let me share you. You
don't mind staying a little while?'

She shook her head. 'Not in the least. I'll stay as long as you want me to.'

He snorted. 'Don't let us wrap up our words. You know as well as I do that I shall probably be dead in a week or so. You're not bored?'

It was difficult to answer that, because she was, just a little. She longed to get away for an hour or so each day; she had known that she would spend some time with Jonkheer van der Blocq each day, but even private nurses were entitled to their free periods, and she wasn't a private nurse—Fabian had told her that. He had spoken of trips to Groningen and getting a mount from the nearby stables; so far she had had no time for either, indeed she had no idea where the stables were, and when, on the previous day, she had mentioned going for a walk to Freule van der Blocq, that good lady had reacted quite violently to the suggestion; it seemed that the idea of being left with her father was more than she could bear, so Mary Jane had said no more about it. When Doctor Trouw paid his next visit, she would have a little talk with him and see what could be done.

She had hoped that Fabian would have come, even for half an hour to see how she was managing, but although the telephone rang frequently, she had no means of knowing if any of the calls were from him; it was really rather mean of him, and she decided that she liked him even less than she had supposed, and told herself forcefully that she didn't care if she never saw him again.

He came the very next morning, while Mary Jane,

after a protracted argument between her host and his
daughter, was in church. Emma went to church each
Sunday, driven by Jaap in the Mercedes Benz which
was housed, along with a Mini, in the garage at the
back of the house, and she had seen no reason why
Mary Jane shouldn't accompany her. 'Jaap will be
here,' she had pointed out to her enraged parent, 'he
can help you dress and we shall be back very shortly.'

Her father pointed out testily that if Jaap drove
them to church, there would be no one to dress him,
and he certainly wasn't going to wait while Jaap
drove around the countryside just because she wanted
to go to church.

Mary Jane, feeling a little like a bone between two
dogs, felt her patience wearing thin round the edges.
'Look,' she offered when she could make herself
heard 'can't I drive the Mini? It's no distance, and
that would leave Jaap free.'

So they had gone to church and on the return journey when she turned the little car carefully into the
drive once more, it was to find a silver-grey pre-war
Jaguar SS 100 parked before the door. She got out
and went to inspect it with a good deal of interest; it
wasn't an original but a modern version of it, she
discovered as she prowled around its chassis, wondering to whom it belonged, and when Cousin Emma
cried happily: 'Oh, good, Fabian's here—this is his
car,' Mary Jane, her inquisitive person bent double
over the dashboard, remarked:

'I don't believe it.'

'Why not?' It was Fabian who spoke and startled

her so much that she turned round in a kind of jump, and when she didn't speak, he repeated impatiently, 'Why not?'

'Well,' she said slowly, 'it's unexpected—I hardly thought that you…'

'I'm too old for it?' His voice was suave.

'What nonsense, of course not, it's just that…' She gave up, staring at him silently. After a moment he laughed and turned to his cousin.

'Well, Emma, how are you? I've been with Oom Georgius. He seems in fine shape, considering all things, though a little annoyed because Mary Jane wasn't at home.'

He looked at Mary Jane as he spoke, and she, aware of his faintly accusing tone, went red, just as though, she thought crossly, she were in the habit of tearing off for hours at a time, whereas the morning's outing, if it could be called that, had been the first since she had arrived. She turned on her heel and walked into the house as Cousin Emma burst into voluble speech.

She was in Jonkheer van de Blocq's room fighting her usual battle over his pills when Fabian came in. He sat down by the fire without speaking, watching her while, with cunning and guile, she persuaded the old man to swallow them down. He still said nothing as she prepared to leave them, only walking to the door to open it for her. She barely glanced at him as she passed through.

They all lunched together in the dining room, and Jonkheer van der Blocq, a little excited at Fabian's

visit, talked a great deal, repeating himself frequently
and forgetting his words and showing little flashes of
splendid rage when he did. The meal took some time
and when it was at last finished he was tired, so that
for once, when Mary Jane suggested that he might
like to lie down for half an hour, he agreed meekly.
She accompanied him upstairs again, tucked him up
on the chaise-longue in his room, thoughtfully provided him with a book, his spectacles, the bell and
the tin of fruit drops he liked to suck, bade him be a
good boy in a motherly voice, and went downstairs.

She was crossing the hall when she heard Fabian's
voice, usually so quiet and measured in its tones,
raised in anger and as she reached the door she could
hear Cousin Emma doing what she described to herself as a real Sarah Bernhardt. Her hand on the heavy
brass knob, she wondered if she should go in, and
had her mind made up for her by a particularly loud
squawk. At any moment, she thought to herself vex-
edly, she would have strong hysterics to deal with,
thanks to Fabian. She flung open the door to find
Freule van der Blocq standing in a tragic pose in the
middle of the room, and Fabian lounging against one
of the Corinthian pillars which supported the vast fire-
place. He spoke sharply.

'There you are! Perhaps you can answer my questions without weeping and wailing. Have you been
out at all since you arrived here?'

'Oh yes—to church.'

'Don't infuriate me, I beg of you, you know very

well what I mean. Have you had time to yourself each day, to go out, to ride, to visit Groningen?'

'Well I...'

'Yes or no?' he ground out.

'You see...'

'I see nothing, largely owing to your inability to answer my questions.' He frowned at her. 'There seems to be some gross misunderstanding; you are here as a guest, to give some time and company to Uncle Georgius at your grandfather's request. That does not mean that you have to spend each day cooped up in the house at everyone's beck and call.'

'Don't exaggerate,' Mary Jane told him calmly, 'just because you're annoyed. It's your fault anyway. You should have explained exactly what I was supposed to do—you didn't tell me much, did you, and I dare say you didn't tell Freule van der Blocq anything either. I refuse to be blamed, and I won't allow you to blame her either.'

He gave her a hard stare. 'Oh? Am I supposed to apologise to you, then?' his voice was silky and very quiet.

'No, I don't suppose any such thing, because I can't imagine you apologising to anyone, though you could at least say you're sorry to your cousin. It's unkind of you to make her cry.'

His eyes had become black, he was still staring at her, rather as though he had never seen her before, she thought uneasily. She shook off the feeling and prompted him, 'Well, go on—or perhaps you would rather not do with me here.'

She whisked out of the room before he could reply and crossed the hall to the long drawing room, a very much gilded apartment, with a wealth of grand furniture and huge display cabinets full of silver and porcelain. Not at all to her taste; she hurried over the vast carpeted floor and into the verandah room beyond where there was a piano. With the doors shut she was sure no one could hear her playing, and really, she had to do something to take her mind off things. It was a beautiful instrument. She sat down on the stool before it and tried a scale with the soft pedal down and then went on to a rambling mixture of tunes, just as they came into her head. She played tolerably well, disregarding wrong notes and forgetting about the soft pedal but putting in a good deal of feeling. Halfway through a half remembered bit of *Eine Kleine Nachtmusik,* Fabian stalked in, taking her by surprise because he entered by the garden door behind her. She stopped at once, folded her hands tidily in her lap and waited to hear what he had to say.

'You are the most infuriating girl!' he began in a pleasantly conversational tone. 'I have apologised to my cousin; if I apologise to you will you be kind enough to listen to what I have to say?'

'Of course—though why...'

'Just listen. I apologise for a start, and now to other matter. It seems that Cousin Emma was so glad to have someone in the house who could handle my uncle that she took advantage of that fact. Unintentionally, I should add. In future you are to take what time you wish for yourself. I know that I can depend upon you to do what you can for Uncle Georgius if and when he becomes worse—I imagine Trouw will give you good warning of that, if it is possible. You are free to go where you wish, is that understood? Have you any money?'

'Not much.'

'I will arrange for you to have sufficient for your needs. I will also see Uncle Georgius and explain to him.'

Mary Jane got up and closed the piano. 'You won't upset him? He's such a dear, I like him.'

He gave her a considering look. 'So do I. If you care to do so, I will drive you over to the riding stables in half an hour and arrange for you to hire a mount.'

'I should like that—are we going in that Jag?'

Fabian looked surprised. 'Of course.' He opened the door and they went through together. 'You play well.'

'Thank you—I hope no one minds.'

'No one will mind.' They were in the hall again, where he left her to go to his uncle's room, and she went into the sitting room where his cousin greeted her in a melodramatic manner and a fresh flood of tears. She was still eulogising Fabian, Mary Jane and then Fabian again when the object of her praise walked in, bidding Mary Jane to fetch her coat and go with him—something she was glad to do, for much as she liked Cousin Emma, a little of her went a long way, especially when she was upset.

It was cold in the car, but she had tied her head in a scarf and Fabian had tucked a rug around her. She sat, exhilarated by the fresh air and their progress through the narrow country roads. The stables were a mile or so away; the journey seemed too short; for once Fabian was being pleasant—she allowed him to choose a quiet mare for her use with the secret resolve to pick out something a little more lively once he was safely back in Groningen—there was no use in annoying him over such a small matter, especially as he seemed disposed to be friendly, indeed he seemed in such a good frame of mind that she was emboldened to ask him how his work was going and whether he was still busy.

'Yes, just at the moment, but I shall be able to come over from time to time—in any case, there will be some papers for you to sign in a few days—some stocks I am transferring.' She looked a little blank and he went on smoothly, 'It seems to me to be somewhat of a paradox that you should trust me without question to attend to your affairs while at the same time you dislike me.'

She bit her lip and wished he wouldn't say things she couldn't answer. After a little thought, she said carefully, 'Well, I haven't much choice, have I?' and was annoyed when he laughed.

He went away after tea and she spent most of the evening trying to convince Jonkheer van der Blocq that just because she wanted to go out sometimes it didn't mean that she didn't like his company. She played three games of Racing Demon with him to prove her point.

The best time to go riding was in the morning. Mary Jane had an early breakfast and took the Mini over to the stables and rode for an hour. By the time she got back to the house, her host was awake and clamouring for her and his daughter was wanting her company. It worked very well, for they hardly noticed her absence, and she, refreshed by her morning exercise, felt prepared to be at their disposal for the rest of the day. And Fabian had telephoned each day too, to make sure that she was doing as he had asked, and she had answered truthfully enough that she was riding each day. Time enough to go to Groningen—at present the old gentleman needed her company, so did his daughter. She had no great opinion of herself, but she could see that the two of them rubbed each other up the wrong way, and a third party was necessary for peaceful living.

It was on her third morning's ride that she decided to ask for another horse; the mare was a nice beast, but a little slow. Without actually telling any fibs she managed to imply that Fabian had told her that she might make another choice if she wasn't quite pleased with the mare, and chose a bay, a spirited animal with a rolling eye and a little too big for her. But he went well and now that she had got the lie of the country she knew just where to take him—along the shore of the Leekstermeer, where there were trees and a good deal of undergrowth on either side of the unmade road. It was a dull morning, with the threat of rain—

she had put on two sweaters and plaited her hair so
that it would be out of the way, not caring at all if
she should get wet. She reached the road to the lake
and began to pick a way along the path she saw running beside it, looking about her as she did so. It was
pretty there—not a patch on her own lake at home,
but still charming and peaceful, even though the trees
were bare of leaves and the grass was rough. She and
the bay ambled along, for there was time enough; she
could canter back along the road presently, there
would be no traffic to speak of and there was an ample grass verge if he should get restive.

They were on the point of turning to go back when
she became aware of horse's hooves behind her and
when she turned to look it was to see Fabian astride
a great roan, coming towards her at a canter. He rode
well, she noted. He also looked very angry, she noted
that too, and pulled in the bay with a resigned sigh.

His 'good morning' was icy, so she merely nodded
in reply and waited silently for him to speak.

'I picked out a good little mare for you. Why aren't
you riding her?' Mary Jane considered him thoughtfully. 'Well, I'm capable of choosing a mount, for one
thing. I'm sick to death of you treating me as though
I were a half-witted old maid you can barely bring
yourself to be civil to!' She drew a swelling breath.
'And another thing, you may be my guardian, but you
don't own me. I've a mind of my own.'

'And a temper, I see,' he observed dampingly.
'You forget that I had no notion of how you rode. If
I had allowed you to choose for yourself and you

could barely sit the beast and had taken a tumble, I
should have done less than my duty to you as your
guardian.'

'Oh, pooh!' she tossed her head and the pigtail
swung over her shoulder.

'You look about ten years old,' he said unexpectedly, and smiled at her, 'Shall we cry a temporary
truce? I came out to see you; I have those papers
ready for you to sign and I wondered if you would
like to come to Groningen for an hour or so.'

She eyed him with surprise. 'You mean you actually want me to go with you to Groningen?'

His voice was tinged with impatience. 'Yes. You
see I'm being civil. We might even manage not to
quarrel for a couple of hours.' He spoke without smiling now, his face turned away.

'Oh, very well,' she told him, knowing that her
voice sounded ungracious, 'then I'd better go back.'

They rode back in silence. Only when they reached
the stables did Fabian tell her quietly, 'I was mistaken, Mary Jane. You ride well.'

CHAPTER FOUR

FABIAN HAD COME in the Jaguar, so that Mary Jane, with an eye to the weather, tied a silk scarf over her head in place of the unbecoming hat, wishing she had had the sense to bring her sheepskin jacket with her. It was barely November but already cold, and an open car, although great fun, needed suitable clothes, but once they were on their way, she didn't feel cold at all; she glowed with excitement and pleasure. An outing would be delightful, especially if they could remain friends for an hour.

Her patient, in a mellow mood, had agreed to his daughter keeping him company for a short time, only begging Mary Jane to return at the earliest possible moment. His daughter had been rather more urgent in her request not to be left for longer than was absolutely necessary with her irascible parent; she had also given Mary Jane a shopping list of things which she declared she urgently needed. It was a miscellany of knitting wool, embroidery silks, Gentlemen's Relish, chocolate biscuits and a particular brand of bottled peach which could only be obtained at a certain shop in the city. Mary Jane accepted it obligingly, to have it taken from her at once by Fabian, who put it in his pocket with a brisk 'I'll see to these,' and an injunction to hurry herself up. So here she was, sitting snugly beside Fabian, who was making short work of the few miles to Groningen.

She found the city very fine, with its two big squares and its old buildings. Fabian, going slowly through the traffic, pointed out the imposing, towering spire of St Martin's church before he turned off the main street and into a tree-lined one, bisected by a canal. The houses here were patrician, flat-faced and massive, each of them with its great front door reached by a double flight of steps. The sound of the traffic came faintly down its length so that it was easy to hear the rustle of the wind in the trees' bare branches.

'This is beautiful,' declared Mary Jane with satisfaction.

Fabian stopped before one of the houses. 'Yes, I think so too. I'm glad you like it.'

'Is this the lawyer's house?' she asked him.

'No, it's mine. We'll go inside and get those papers dealt with.'

She hadn't thought much about where he lived and when she had, it had been a vague picture of some smallish town house. This mansion took her by surprise, and she was still more surprised when they went inside. The hall was long and narrow and panelled waist high, with rich red carpeting on its floor to cover the black and white of its marble. The wall chandeliers were exquisite and there were flowers on the wall table. She wanted to take a more leisurely look, but an elderly woman appeared from the back of the house, was introduced as Mevrouw Hol and swept her away to an elegantly appointed cloakroom, where she tidied her hair, did things to her face and left her outdoor things before being led to a room close by where Fabian was waiting for her.

She took it to be a study, as it was lined with book-shelves and its main furniture was a massive desk and an equally massive chair, but the chairs by the fire were of a comfortably normal size. Mary Jane took the one offered her and sighed with content; the room was warm and light and airy and quite, quite different from the over-furnished house in which Fabian's uncle lived.

He sat down at the desk now, saying: 'You won't mind having coffee here? We can see to these papers at the same time, they'll not take long.'

She drank her coffee and then, under his direction, signed the papers, each one of which he carefully explained to her before asking her to do so. When she had finished she said with faint apology, 'I'm sorry you've had all this extra work, but I suppose once it's seen to, you won't need to bother, any more.'

'On the contrary.' He didn't smile as he spoke and she felt chilled. 'If you have finished your coffee perhaps you would like to come with me and get Emma's shopping—and by the way, I believe that I promised you some money for your own use.' He opened a drawer in the desk and handed her a little bundle of notes. 'There are a thousand gulden there. If you need more, please ask me.'

She looked at him round-eyed. 'Whatever should I want with all that money?'

He smiled faintly. 'I imagine that you will find things to buy with it.'

She became thoughtful. 'Well, yes—there are one or two things…'

He went back to his desk and silently handed her a pad and pencil. A few minutes later she looked up. 'You know,' she informed him in surprise, 'I've made quite a list.'

'I thought maybe you would. Would a store suit you or do you want a boutique?'

She shot him a suspicious glance which he countered with a grave detachment. How did he know about boutiques? she wondered, and assured him that a large store would be much easier. 'I'll be as quick as I can, she assured him.

'No need—I told Cousin Emma that we shouldn't be back until after tea. We'll lunch out and you will have hours of time.'

Mary Jane had forgotten how pleasant it was to go shopping with plenty of money to spend. By the time Fabian had worked his way through the list Emma had given them, it was burning a hole in her purse, and when Fabian left her outside a large store, assuring her that most of the assistants spoke English and she had nothing to worry about and that he would be waiting for her in an hour's time, she could hardly wait to start on a tour of inspection. Fabian had been right, there was no difficulty in making herself understood; everyone seemed to speak English. She bought everything which she had written on her list and a good deal besides, and when, strolling through the hat department, she saw a velvet beret which would go very well with her coat, she bought that too and, a little drunk with the success of her shopping, put it on.

She was only ten minutes late at the store entrance and when she would have apologised to Fabian for keeping him waiting he said to surprise her, 'Late? Are you? I never expected you back within the hour and a half—we agreed upon an hour, if you remember. We'll have lunch and if you have anything else to buy you can get it later.'

They lunched at the Hotel Baulig, and as they were both hungry they started the meal with *erwtensoep*— a thick pea soup enriched with morsels of bacon and ham and sausage, went on to a dish of salmon with asparagus tips and quenelles of sole, and having finished this delicacy, agreed upon fresh fruit salad to round off their lunch. They sat a considerable time over their coffee, for rather to Mary Jane's surprise, they found plenty to talk about, and although she thought Fabian rather reserved in his manner, at least he was agreeable.

They did a little more shopping after they left the hotel, for it seemed sense to her to buy one or two presents while she had the opportunity. It was when she had declared herself satisfied with her purchases that Fabian remarked, 'But you have bought nothing for yourself.'

'Yes, I have, lots of things—and a hat.' She waited for him to notice the beret and was deeply mortified when he said: 'Oh, did you? why don't you wear it, then?' He glanced at their parcels. 'It must be a very small one, there's nothing here which looks like a hat bag.'

She boiled, but silently. She wasn't sure if he was teasing her or if he took so little notice of her that he hadn't even noticed what she was wearing. Neither of these ideas were very complimentary to herself. She answered with a sweetness which any of her closer friends would have suspected, 'I know where it is. I think I've finished, thank you. I expect you would like to be getting back to Midwoude.'

He gave her a searching look. 'Why?'

'Well, you've done your good deed for today, haven't you?' Her voice was light despite his look.

'Indeed yes, and it's made me thirsty. Shall we have tea somewhere?'

She kept her voice light. 'No, thank you. I think I should like to go back now. I'm most grateful to you...'

His tone was curt. 'Spare the thanks,' he begged her coldly, and thereafter sustained an ultra-polite conversation during their short journey back to Mid- woude where he handed her and her packages over to Jaap, wished her a distant good evening, got back into his car and drove away, a great deal too fast.

Emma van der Blocq, pouring a late tea in the small room at the back of the house where the two of them sometimes sat, professed surprise as Mary Jane joined her. 'I didn't expect you back until much later,' she declared happily, 'but surely Fabian could have stayed for tea—even for dinner?' She interrupted herself. 'No, perhaps not for dinner—he goes out a good deal, you know. Where did you have lunch, Mary Jane?'

She remembered the name of the hotel and felt rather pleased with herself about it, and Cousin Emma nodded, her interest aroused.

'A very nice place. Of course he really prefers the Hotel at Warffrum—Borg de Breedenburg—but that is for his more romantic outings.' She smiled at Mary Jane. 'He has girl-friends, as you can imagine—I wonder why he didn't take you there?'

'I imagine,' said Mary Jane in a dry little voice, 'that I don't qualify for a romantic background.'

'No, perhaps not,' agreed her companion with disconcerting directness. 'Fabian only takes out very pretty girls, you know—and always beautifully dressed, as you can imagine.' She smiled again, quite oblivious of any feelings Mary Jane might possess. 'He's a most observant man.'

'You surprise me,' said Mary Jane waspishly, thinking of the lovely velvet beret he hadn't even noticed. 'And now I'll just go up and see how Jonkheer van der Blocq is. Did he have a quiet day?'

Her companion's face crumpled ominously. 'Oh, my dear, however did I manage before you came? He was so cross, and he refused to take his pills. Doctor Trouw will be here presently and he will be so annoyed.' She sounded so upset that Mary Jane paused on her way to the door.

'He's far too nice to get cross with you,' she assured her, 'and he knows that it isn't always easy…'

Emma's face broke into a simper. 'Oh yes, he is so good... I've known him for years, you know, long before he married. His wife died last year. She was a quiet little thing—no looks at all. You remind me of her.'

To which remark Mary Jane could think of no answer at all. She escaped through the door and spent the rest of the evening with the old gentleman, who seemed delighted to see her again and to her great relief made no remarks at all about her face or her lack of looks.

It turned a great deal colder the next day, but Mary Jane went riding just the same, bundled in several sweaters against the wind, and returning to the house with glowing cheeks and a sparkle in her eyes. Of Fabian there was no sign, but that didn't surprise her—why should he come anyway? He had only visited the house because he needed some papers signed—it certainly wasn't for her company. Let him use his leisure escorting the beauties of Groningen to romantic dinners, she thought, her lip curling, and then her mood changed and she fell to thinking how very satisfactory it would be if she could be escorted to this hotel Emma had been so enthusiastic about, wearing the organza dress. She sighed and prodded her mount to quicken his pace. Chance was a fine thing, she told him, as they turned for home.

She had her chance the very next day, as it turned out, for when Doctor Trouw called he brought his son with him. A pleasant young man in his twenties, he had recently qualified and was about to join his father's practice. Over coffee he remarked, 'You are stranger here, I don't suppose you go out very much. I should like to take you out to dinner one evening.'

Mary Jane accepted with alacrity, and when, to her delight, he suggested that he should take her to Hotel Borg de Breedenborg on the following evening, she agreed with flattering speed.

She spent the intervening time imagining herself sweeping into the restaurant while Fabian, already there with some girl, would be bowled over by the sight of her in the organza, prettied up for the evening. The urge to shake him out of his cool, casual attitude towards herself was growing very strong, it caused her to take twice as long as usual in her preparations for the evening, which were so effective that when she went along to see her patient before they left, he was constrained to remark upon her changed appearance, as indeed was Cousin Emma, who rather tactlessly remarked that she hardly recognised Mary Jane in her finery.

Willem was rather nice and she was determined to have a pleasant evening. As they drove to the hotel she set herself to draw him out with a few well-chosen questions about his work. It wasn't until they reached the hotel that she was struck by the thought that her chance of seeing Fabian was small indeed. Even if he had a host of girl-friends, he surely didn't dine there every evening. He had his work—presumably that kept him busy, and surely he must spend some of his evenings at home, catching up on his reading, writing, even operating when it was necessary. She left her coat, patted the hair which had taken so long to put up and determinedly dismissed him from her head as she rejoined Willem.

The restaurant was full and she realized with something of a shock that it was already Saturday again—a whole week since she had seen Fabian. She sat down opposite her companion, gave him a brilliant smile and glanced around her. Fabian was sitting quite near their table, and the girl he was with was just as lovely as she had imagined she would be. Mary Jane turned the brilliance of her smile into a polite, tight-lipped one as she caught his eye and turned her attention to Willem, who, once they had ordered, launched into an earnest description of his days, hour by hour, almost minute by minute. She strove to keep an interested expression on her face, and when it was possible, laughed gaily, so that Fabian, whom she hadn't looked at again, would see how much she was enjoying herself. It was a pity that Fabian and his companion should go while they themselves were only half way through dinner. He paused as they passed the table, his hand on the girl's arm. He said austerely, 'I'm glad to see that you are enjoying yourself, Mary Jane,' nodded briefly to Willem and went on his way. Mary Jane watched him smile down at the girl as they went through the door and then wondered briefly where they were going, and then concentrated on Willem, who had started to tell her at great length about a girl he had met at his hospital. She obviously occupied his thoughts to a large extent; by the time he had finished, Mary Jane even knew the size of her shoes.

They went back to the house at a reasonable hour because, as Willem reminded her, his father, who was dining with Cousin Emma and keeping an eye on her father at the same time, needed a good night's sleep. He took his farewell of her half an hour later with the hope that they might spend another evening together before she returned to England, and Mary Jane, thanking him nicely, wondered how she could possibly have been interested in him, even for such a short time; he was so very worthy, and looking back on their evening she could remember no conversation at all on her part, merely a succession of 'really's' and 'fancy that's' and 'you don't say so's'. When he and his father had gone she gave Cousin Emma a potted version of her evening because she could see that the lady had no intention of allowing her to go to bed until she had done so, and then she went to Jonkheer van der Blocq's room to see if he had settled for the night. Somehow or other, he had contrived not to take his sleeping tablet, which necessitated her arguing gently with him for the best part of ten minutes, but when he had finally consented to do as she asked and she had turned his pillows and settled him nicely, he enquired after her evening, observing in no uncertain manner that he found Willem a dull fellow, which naturally had the effect of her replying that he had been a very interesting companion, that the dinner had been delicious, and that he had asked her out again.

'What did you talk about?' growled the old man.

'Oh, his work, naturally. And a girl he met while he was in hospital—he's very taken with her. He—talked a lot about her.'

Jonkheer van der Blocq laughed until he had no breath. Mary Jane gave him a drink, told him severely that there was nothing to laugh about, wished him good night and presently went to bed herself. She hadn't mentioned to anyone that Fabian had been at the hotel too, and she didn't think she would.

He came the next morning while they were in church, and this time it was the Rolls parked outside the door when they returned. As they went in he came downstairs, wished them a pleasant good morning, agreed that a cup of coffee would be welcome and when Emma had disappeared kitchenwards to find someone to make it, turned to Mary Jane and invited her to enter the sitting room.

'I'll take my things upstairs first,' she told him coldly, and was frustrated by his instant offer to take her coat, which he tossed on to a chair.

'It can stay there for a moment,' he told her rather impatiently. 'I see you are wearing the new hat. It's pretty—so you found it.'

She gave him a frosty look and said witheringly, 'It wasn't difficult, it was on my head.'

The dark wings of his brows soared. 'Oh dear—I can see that I must apologise, my dear girl, and I do. I could make a flowery speech, but you would make mincemeat of it, so I'll just say that I'm sorry.'

She walked away from him into the sitting room, where she sat down, telling herself indignantly that she didn't care if he followed her or not. He took the chair opposite hers and stretched his long legs and studied her carefully.

'You wouldn't believe me if I say how charming you looked yesterday evening?' he asked mildly.

'No.' She added nastily, 'You haven't a clue as to what I was wearing.'

His smile mocked her. 'Sea green, or would you call it sea blue, something thin and silky. It had long sleeves with frills over your wrists and a frill under your chin and a row of buttons down the back of the bodice.'

She was astounded, but she managed to say with a tinge of sarcasm:

'A photographic eye, I see,' and then because her female curiosity had got the better of her good sense. 'The girl you were with was lovely.'

He picked a tiny thread from a well-tailored sleeve. 'Delightfully so. She wears a different wig every day of the week and the longest false eyelashes I have ever seen.'

Mary Jane turned a chuckle into a cough. 'And why not? It's the fashion. Besides, she would look gorgeous in anything she chose to put on.'

He agreed placidly. 'And you found William Trouw entertaining?' he asked suavely.

'We had a very pleasant evening,' she told him guardedly.

'A worthy young man,' went on her companion ruminatively. 'He would make a good husband—do you fancy him?'

She choked. 'Well, of all the things to say! I've been out with him once, and here you are, talking as though...'

He went on just as though she had never interrupted him. 'He has a good practice with his father, so he wouldn't be after your money, and I imagine he has all the attributes of a good husband—good-natured, no interest in drinking or betting, or girls, for that matter—a calm disposition, he...'

She ground her teeth. 'Be quiet! You may be my guardian, but you shan't talk like that. I'll marry whom I please and when I want to, and until then you can mind your own business!'

'From which outburst I conclude that Willem hasn't won your heart?'

She wanted to laugh, but she choked it back. 'No, he hasn't. As a matter of fact he spent quite a long time telling me about a girl he knew in hospital. I think he intends to marry her.'

'Ah, I wondered what it was that you found so interesting, though surely it was unkind of you to laugh so much during the recital?'

'I didn't...' she began, and stopped, because of course she had, so that Fabian should think she was having a lovely time. 'I enjoyed myself very much,' she muttered peevishly, and was glad to see Cousin Emma and Jaap with the coffee tray, coming into the room.

Fabian stayed for lunch, and his uncle insisted upon coming down to join them, contributing to the conversation with such gusto that Mary Jane feared for

his blood pressure. But at least he was so tired after
his meal that she had no difficulty in persuading him
to take his customary nap, and when she had tucked
him up and come downstairs again it was to find that
Emma had allowed herself to be driven over to Doctor Trouw's house for tea. Which left her and Fabian.
He was waiting for her in the hall and he sounded
impatient.

'Shall we have a walk before tea?'

Mary Jane paused at the bottom of the staircase.
'Thank you, no. I have letters to write.'

'Which you can write at any time.' He came towards her. 'It's not often I'm here.'

'Oh—should I mind?'

'Don't be an impudent girl, and don't imagine it is
because I want your company,' he added quite violently. 'I had a letter from Mr North asking me to
explain certain aspects of your inheritance to you, so
I might just as well do it and take some exercise at
the same time.'

'Charming!' observed Mary Jane, her eyes snap-
ping with temper, 'and so good of you to fit me in
with one of your more healthy activities.'

'And what,' he asked awfully, 'exactly do you
mean by that remark?'

'Just exactly what I say. I'll come for half an
hour—in that time you should be able to tell me whatever I'm supposed to know.'

She crossed the hall and picked up her coat, caught
up her gloves and went to the pillow cupboard, rum-
maged around in its depths until she found a scarf

which she tied carelessly over her hair. 'Ready,' she said with a distinct snap.

They walked away from the village, into the teeth of a mean wind, while Fabian talked about stocks and shares and gilt-edged securities and capital gains tax to all of which she lent only half an ear. As far as she could see she would have a perfectly adequate income whatever he and Mr North decided to do with her money. As long as she had sufficient to run the house and pay for Mrs Body and Lily and have some over to run the car and buy clothes... She stopped suddenly and told him so.

'You are not only a tiresome girl, you are also a very ungrateful one,' Fabian informed her bitterly.

'I'm sorry—about being ungrateful, I mean, but I can't remember being tiresome—was it on any particular occasion?'

He sounded quite weary. 'You are tiresome all the time,' he told her, which surprised her so much that she walked in silence until he observed that since she wished to return to Midwoude within half an hour, they had better go back. They didn't speak at all, and in the hall they parted. When Mary Jane came downstairs ten minutes later, it was to find that he had gone. She told herself with a little surge of rage that it was a good thing too, for when they were together they did nothing but disagree. She wandered across to the sitting room, telling herself again, this time out loud, that she was delighted, and added the hope that she wouldn't see him for simply ages.

But it wasn't simply ages, it was the following

Wednesday, or rather three o'clock on Thursday morning. Jonkheer van der Blocq had had, for him, a very good day. They had played their usual game of cards, and she had helped him to bed, just a little worried because his colour was bad. But Doctor Trouw had called that afternoon, and although the old gentleman was failing rapidly now, he had seen no cause for immediate alarm. Mary Jane went to bed early, first taking another look at her patient. He was asleep, and there was nothing to justify her unease.

The peal of the bell wakened her. She bundled on her dressing gown, and not waiting to put her feet in slippers, ran across the dim landing. The old man was lying very much as she had left him, but now his colour was livid, although he said with his usual irascibility, 'I feel most peculiar—I want Fabian here at once.'

She murmured soothingly while she took a frighteningly weak pulse and studied his tired old face before she went to the telephone. It was quite wrong to ring up in front of the patient, but she didn't dare leave him. She rang Doctor Trouw first, with a suitably guarded request for him to come, and then dialled Fabian's number. His voice, calm and clear over the line, gave her the instant feeling that she didn't need to worry about anything because he was there— she forgot that they weren't on speaking terms, that he was arrogant and treated her like a tiresome child. She said simply, 'Oh, Fabian—will you come at once? Your uncle'—she paused, aware that the bed's occupant was listening—'would like to speak to you,' she finished.

'He's listening?'

'Yes.'

'I'll be with you in fifteen minutes. Get Trouw.'

'I have.'

'Good girl! Get Jaap up and tell him to open the gates and the door. Get Emma up too—no, wait—tell Jaap to do that. You stay with my uncle.'

She said, 'Yes, Fabian,' and put down the receiver. 'Fabian's on his way,' she told Jonkheer van der Blocq in a calm, reassuring voice. 'I'm to wake Jaap so that he can open the gates. Stay just as you are— I'll only be few moments.'

Doctor Trouw came a few minutes later, and in response to the old gentleman's demand to be given something to keep him going, gave him an injection, told him to save his breath in the understanding voice of an old friend and went to Emma's room, where she could be heard crying very loudly.

Mary Jane pulled up a chair to the bedside, tucked her cold feet under her and took Jonkheer van der Blocq's hand in hers. 'Fabian won't be long,' she told him again, because she sensed that was what he wanted above anything else. She certainly was justified, because a moment later she heard the soft, powerful murmur of the Rolls' engine and the faint crunch of its tyres as Fabian stopped outside the front door.

He entered the room without haste, wearing a thick sweater and slacks and looking very wide awake. He said: 'Hullo, Uncle Georgius,' and nodded to Mary

Jane, his dark, bright gaze taking in the dressing-gown, the plaited hair and her bare feet. He said kindly, 'What a girl you are for forgetting your slippers! Go and put them on, it's cold, and tell Trouw I'm here, will you. I don't suppose he heard me come, with the row Emma's making.'

His uncle made a weak, explosive sound. 'Silly woman,' he said, in a voice suddenly small, 'always crying—you'll keep an eye on her, Fabian?'

'Of course.' He lapsed into Dutch as Mary Jane reached the door.

Emma was in no state to be left alone; Mary Jane stayed with her as Doctor Trouw hurried across the landing, and was still with her when he came back to tell them that his patient was dead. It wasn't until poor Emma had had something to send her to sleep, and Mary Jane had tucked her up in bed, that she felt free to leave her.

The old house was very quiet; there was a murmur of voices coming from the kitchen, and still more voices behind the closed door of the small sitting room. She stood in the hall, wondering if she should go back to bed, a little uncertain as to what Doctor Trouw might expect of her. It was chilly in the hall and the tick-tock of the over-elaborate French grandfather dripped into the stillness with an oily sloth which she found intensely irritating. A cup of tea would have been nice, she thought despondently, and turned to go back upstairs just as the sitting room door opened and Fabian said: 'Ah, there you are. Come in—Jaap's bringing tea.' He glanced at her pale face.

'You look as though you need it. Cousin Emma's asleep?'

She nodded, then sat down in a chair by the still burning fire and drank her tea, listening to the two men talking and saying very little herself. When she had finished she got to her feet. 'Is there anything you would like me to do?' she asked.

Doctor Trouw shook his head. 'The district nurse will be here very shortly. Go to bed, Mary Jane, and get some sleep. I am most grateful to you for all you have done and I will ask you to do something else. Would you look after Emma for a few days? She has very sensitive nature and I am afraid this will be too much for her—I will leave something for her, if you will give it when she wakes, and be round about lunch time to see how she is.'

She nodded, thinking that Cousin Emma would be even more difficult than her father, and went to the door which Fabian had opened for her. He followed her into the hall, shutting the door behind him, and she turned round tiredly to see what he wanted.

His voice was quiet. 'I know what you are thinking. We have imposed upon you and we have no right but I too would be grateful if you would stay just for little while and help Emma—she likes you and she needs you.'

She said shortly, 'Oh, that's all right. Of course I'll stay.

He came nearer. 'You have had a lot to bear in the last few weeks, Mary Jane. Once I called you a tiresome girl. I apologise.' He bent and kissed her cheek with a gentleness which disturbed her more than any of the harsh words he had uttered in the past. She went upstairs, not answering his good night.

The next few days were a peculiar medley of intense activity, doing all the things Cousin Emma insisted should be done; receiving visitors, whose hushed voices and platitudes caused her to sit in floods of tears for hours after they had gone; going to Groningen to buy the black garments she considered essential and relating, seemingly endlessly, her father's perfections to Mary Jane, while crying herself sick again.

Mary Jane found it all a little difficult to stomach—father and daughter had hardly had a happy relationship while he was alive, now that he was dead he had somehow become a kind of saint. But she liked Emma, although she found her histrionics a little trying, and she did what she could to keep her as calm as possible, addressed countless envelopes and kept out of Fabian's way as much as possible.

He came frequently, but her quick ears, tuned to the gentle hum of the Rolls-Royce or the exuberant roar of the Jaguar, gave her warning enough to slip away while he was in the house. But one evening she had made the mistake of supposing that he had left the house; it was almost dinner time and there was no sound of voices from either of the sitting rooms. He must have gone, she decided, while she had been up in the attic, packing away Jonkheer van der Blocq's clothes until such time as his daughter found herself capable of deciding what to do with them. The

small sitting room was dimly lit by the firelight and
one lamp, and Freule van der Blocq was lying asleep
on the sofa. Fabian was on one of the easy chairs, his
legs thrust out before him, contemplating the ceiling,
but he got up as Mary Jane started to leave the room
as silently and quickly as she had entered it. Outside
in the hall he demanded: 'Where have you been?'

'Upstairs in the attics, sorting your uncle's clothes.'

'Have you, by God? Surely there's someone else
to such work? And that was not what I meant. Where
have you been? Whenever I come, I am conscious of
your disappearing footsteps. Do you dislike me so
much?'

She eyed him thoughtfully. 'I never think about it,'
she said at length, not quite truthfully.

His expressive eyebrows rose. 'No? You thought I
had gone?'

'Yes.'

He grinned. 'I'm staying to dinner, and now you're
here there's no point in retreating, is there? We'll
have a glass of sherry.'

She accompanied him to the big sitting room and
sat down composedly while he poured their drinks.
When he had settled himself near her he asked,
'When do you want to go home?'

'I should like to go as soon as the funeral is over.
I understand that Emma is going away the day after—
I could leave at the same time.' She sipped her sherry.
'If you would be kind enough to let me have some
more money, I can see about getting my ticket.'

'No need. I shall take you with the car.'

She kept her voice reasonable. 'I don't want to go in your car. I'm quite capable of looking after myself, you know. Besides, you have your work.' She looked at him, saw his smouldering gaze bent upon her and added hastily, 'I'm very grateful, but I can't let you waste any more time on me.'

'Have I ever complained that I was wasting my time on you?'

'No—but one senses these things.'

He gave a crack of laughter. 'One might be mistaken. Would you feel better about it if I told you that I have to go over to England anyway within the next few days—I'm only offering you a lift.'

She said doubtfully, 'Really? Well, that's different, I'll be glad to go with you.'

She missed the gleam in his eyes. 'Tuesday, then. Cousin Emma will be fetched by her friends after breakfast. I'll come for you about four o'clock. I've a ward round to do in the morning and a couple of patients to see after that. We'll go from Rotterdam, I think straight to Hull.' He thought for a minute. 'If we leave here after tea we shall have plenty of time to catch the ferry at Europort. If I'm not here by half past four, have tea and be ready to leave, will you?'

'Certainly.'

'You'll want to telephone Mrs Body.' He strolled across the room and picked up the receiver from the telephone on the delicate serpentine table between the windows. 'What is the number?'

It was nice to hear Mrs Body's motherly voice again. Mary Jane listened to her comfortable com-

ments and felt a wave of homesickness sweep over
her. It would be lovely to be home again. She told
Mrs Body her news and heard that lady's voice asking
if the dear doctor would be staying. Mary Jane hadn't
thought about that. She repeated the enquiry and he
turned to look at her. 'I began to think you weren't
going to ask me,' he remarked mildly. 'A day or so,
if I may.'

Mrs Body sighed in a satisfied manner when Mary
Jane told her. 'That will be nice,' she said as she rang
off, leaving Mary Jane wondering how much truth
there was in that remark. Probably they would quarrel
again before his visit was over, and there was nothing
nice about that.

But at least they didn't quarrel that evening, tacit
consent, they allied to keep Cousin Emma interested
and amused, and succeeded so well that she didn't
cry once and went to bed quite cheerful. Mary Jane,
quite tired herself, went to bed early too and closed
her eyes on the thought that when Fabian wished, he
could be a most agreeable companion.

She saw little of him until Tuesday, when Cousin
Emma, vowing eternal thanks, was packed off to stay
with her friends and Mary Jane found herself alone
in the house except for Jaap and the cook. The morning passed slowly enough because she had nothing
much to do but go for a walk, but after her solitary
lunch she settled down with a book until four o'clock,
when she did her face and hair once more, got Jaap
to bring down her case and went to the window to

watch for the car. It didn't come; it hadn't come by half past four either. She had her tea, punctuated by frequent visits to the window, and when she had finished, put on her outdoor things, made sure that she had every thing with her, and sat down to wait. It was a quarter to six when the car's headlights lighted up the drive. She went into the hall to meet him, saying without any hint of the impatience she felt: 'You'd like a cup of tea, wouldn't you? I asked Jaap to be ready with one.'

'Good girl. I missed lunch—an emergency—I was called back to theatre.'

She was already on her way to the kitchen. 'I'll get some sandwiches.' She paused. 'I hope it was a success.'

'I think so—we shan't be certain for a couple of days.'

She nodded understandingly as she went, to return very soon with a tray of tea and buttered toast, sandwiches and cake. She poured the tea, gave him his toast and sat down again. Presently he said:

'You're very restful—not one reproach for being late, or missing the boat or where have I been.'

'Well, it wouldn't help much if I did, would it?' she wanted to know in a matter-of-fact voice. 'Besides, there's time enough, isn't there? The Rolls goes like a bomb, doesn't she, and the ferry doesn't leave until about midnight.'

'Sensible Miss Pettigrew! But I had planned a leisurely dinner on the way. Now it will have to be a hurried one.'

She smiled at him without malice. 'That won't matter much, will it? Now if I'd been the girl you were with the other night, that would be quite a different kettle of fish...'

He put down his cup slowly. 'You're a great one for the unvarnished truth, aren't you?'

She got up and went over to the big gilt-framed mirror at the opposite end of the room and twitched the beret to a more becoming angle.

'Seeing that we have to deal with each other until I'm thirty,' she said in a tranquil voice, 'we might as well be truthful with each other, even if nothing else.'

'Nothing else what?' He spoke sharply.

She went to pour him a second cup. 'Nothing,' she told him.

They set out shortly afterwards. It was a cold dark evening and the road was almost free of traffic and Fabian sent the car tearing along on the first stage of their journey. He showed no signs of tiredness but sat relaxed behind the wheel—it was a pity it wasn't light, he told her, for they were going to Rotterdam down the other side of the Ijsselmeer, and she would have been able to see a little more of Holland. Mary Jane agreed with him and they sat in silence as they ripped through the flat landscape. Only when they reached Alkmaar and slowed to go through its narrow streets did he say, 'I'm poor company. I'm sorry.'

'The case this afternoon?' she ventured, to be rewarded by his surprised, 'How did you guess? Would it bore you if I told you about it?'

She wasn't bored; she listened with interest and

intelligence and asked the right questions in the right places. They were approaching Rotterdam when he said finally, 'Thank you for listening so well—I can't think of any other girl to whom I would have talked like that.'

She felt a little pang of pure pleasure and tried to think of something to say, but couldn't.

They had their dinner in haste at the Old Dutch restaurant, and Mary Jane, seeing how tired Fabian looked, did her utmost to keep the conversation of a nature which could provoke no difference of opinion between them, and succeeded so well that they boarded the ferry on the friendliest of terms.

The journey was uneventful but rough, but they were both too tired to bother about the weather. They met at breakfast and she was delighted to find that his humour was still a good one. Perhaps now that they wouldn't be seeing much of each other, he was prepared to unbend a little. She accompanied him down to the car deck, hoping that this pleasant state of affairs would last.

It didn't, at least only until they reached the Lakes to receive a rapturous welcome from Mrs Body and sit down to one of her excellent teas. They barely begun the meal when Mary Jane stated, 'I intend to buy a horse tomorrow.'

'No, you won't.' Fabian spoke unhurriedly and with old finality.

She opened her eyes wide. 'Haven't I enough money?' she demanded.

'Don't make ridiculous statements like that—you

have plenty of money. If you want a mount, I'll come with you, and you will allow me to choose the animal.' 'No, I won't! I can ride, you know I can.'

'Nevertheless, you will do as I ask, but before you start spending your money there are one or two details to attend to, I must ask you to come with me to the bank at Keswick, and Mr North will be coming here tomorrow morning. He will bring the last of the papers for you to sign, and as from then your income will be paid into your account each quarter. Should you need more money, you will have to advise me and I will advance it from the estate, should I consider it necessary.'

She boiled with rage. 'Consider it? It's ridiculous—it's like being a child, having to ask you for everything I want!'

He remained unmoved by her outburst. 'How inaccurate you are! You have more than sufficient to live on in comfort, and as long as you keep within your income, you will have no need to apply to me.'

She snorted, 'I should hope not—I'd rather be a pauper!'

'Even more inaccurate.'

There seemed no more to be said; she wasn't disposed to say that she was sorry and she could see that such an intention on his part hadn't even crossed his mind. He excused himself presently and she saw him cleaning the Rolls at the back of the house. From a distance he looked nice. He was a handsome man, she had to admit, and amusing when he wished to be, and kind; only, she told herself darkly, when one got to know him better did one discover what an ill-tempered, arrogant, unsympathetic... She ran out of adjectives.

He stayed two more days, coldly polite, unfailingly courteous and as withdrawn as though they were complete strangers forced to share a small slice of life together. She told herself that she was glad to see him go as the Rolls went through the gate and disappeared down the road to Keswick. He hadn't turned round to wave, either, and he must have known that she was standing in the porch. His goodbye had been casual in the extreme and he had made no mention of their future meeting. Mary Jane stormed back into the house, very put out and banged the door behind her, telling Major in a loud angry voice that life would be heaven without him.

CHAPTER FIVE

IT WAS HEAVEN for three or four days, during which Mary Jane explored the house from attic to cellar, examining with affection the small treasures her grandfather had possessed and which were now hers. She worked in the garden too, sweeping the leaves from the frosty ground, and went walking each day beside the lake with Major. It was cold now, and the snow had crept further down the mountains, but the sun still shone. She drove to Keswick, and to Carlisle to see Mr North, reflecting that it would have been marvelous weather for riding. But she had stubbornly refused to allow Fabian to choose a horse for her, and only after he had pressed the matter had she said that she wouldn't buy one at all if she couldn't have her own way; a decision she was regretting, for she had cut off her nose to spite her face, and a lot of good it had done her.

He hadn't even bothered to write to her—out of sight, out of mind, she muttered bitterly to herself, quite forgetting that she had hardly contributed to increase any desire on his part to have any more to do with her other than businesswise. It was that night, as she lay in bed very much awake, that she made the astonishing discovery that she actually missed him. She examined this from all angles and decided finally that it was because his extreme bossiness had imposed itself far too firmly upon her mind. Well, she was free of him now. She had a house of her own and what seemed to her to be quite a fortune—she could do exactly what she liked, whether he liked it or not—and she would too. She fell asleep making rather wild plans.

She found herself, as the days passed, filling them rather feverishly, quite often doing things which didn't need doing at all, taking walks which became increasingly longer, making excuses to get out the Mini and drive into Cockermouth or Keswick, and although she was happy she was lonely too, missing the rush and bustle of hospital life. In a few short weeks it would be Christmas and she wondered what to do about it. She hadn't a relation in the world whom she knew of and her friends were miles away in London, and what was more, they wouldn't be free over Christmas—nurses seldom were. She wondered what her grandfather and Mrs Body had done in previous years and went to ask that good lady, who chuckled gently and said:

'Well, Miss Mary Jane, not a great deal—your grand-father liked his turkey and his Christmas pudding, and his friends came in for a drink. When he was younger, he used to give a dinner party—even have a few of his closer friends to stay, but they've died or gone away. The last few years have been a bit quiet.' She looked a little wistful. 'I suppose you haven't any friends who could come—a few jolly young people?'

Mary Jane explained about nurses not getting holidays at Christmas and Mrs Body said: 'Well, there's Doctor Morris, and there's Commander Willis—he's a very old friend of your grandfather's, but Lily was telling me that he's not been so well lately...'

They stared at each other, empty of ideas and a little depressed. The sound of a car turning into the drive sent them both into the hall to peer out of the small window beside the front door. 'It'll be that nice Doctor van der Blocq,' breathed Mrs Body happily, 'Oh, how lovely if it is!'

Mary Jane was looking out of the window; if it was keen disappointment she felt when she saw that the car was an Alfa Romeo and the man getting out of it wasn't Fabian, she was quite unaware of it. The man was a stranger, young, fair and not very tall. He seemed to be in no hurry to ring the bell but stood staring at the house and then turned his attention to the garden. Only when he had looked his fill did he advance towards the door. As he rang the bell Mary Jane retreated to the sitting room, waving an urgent hand at Mrs Body. She just had time to sit down in her grandfather's chair and take up the morning paper before the housekeeper, after the shortest of colloquies, put her head round the door. She looked surprised and excited.

'A young gentleman to see you, Miss Mary Jane. Mr Pettigrew from Canada.'

Mary Jane cast down the paper and goggled at her. 'Mr Pettigrew?' Enlightenment struck her. 'Do you suppose he's the cousin—the Canadian cousin—did he say?'

Mrs Body shook her head. 'He wants to see you.'

Mary Jane went into the hall. The young man was standing by the wall table, one of the Georgian candlesticks which rested upon it in his hands, examining it carefully.

She frowned. Even if he were a relation, it was hardly good manners to examine the silver for hallmarks the moment he entered the house. She said coolly, a question in her voice: 'Good morning?'

He put the candlestick down without any trace of embarrassment and crossed the hall, smiling at her, and she found herself smiling back at him, although her first impression of him hadn't been a good one. When he spoke it was with a rich Canadian accent.

'You must think I've got an infernal cheek...' He paused and widened his smile, and Mary Jane, a little on her guard now, allowed her own to fade, but this didn't deter him from continuing: 'I'm a Pettigrew—Mervyn John Pettigrew. My grandfather was your grandfather's cousin—he talked a lot about him when he was alive.' He put a hand into his pocket and withdrew a passport. 'I don't expect you to take me on trust—take a look at this.' And as she stretched out a hand to take it, 'You're Mary Jane, aren't you? I know all about you too.'

She glanced at the passport and gave it back, studying his face. She could see no family likeness, but probably there wouldn't be any; his mother had been a Canadian; he might take after her side of the family.

She said quietly, 'How do you do? Why are you here?'

'We get the English papers—I saw a notice of my great-uncle's death. I had a holiday owing to me, so I decided to fly over and look you up.' He smiled again—he smiled too much, she thought irritably. 'My old man's dead—died two years ago. Mother died when I was a boy, and I'm the only Pettigrew left at home, so I thought I'd look you up.' He gave her a searching glance. 'I don't blame you for not quite believing me, despite the passport. If you'd give me ten minutes, though, I could tell you enough about the family to convince you.'

He had light eyes, a little too close together, but his look was direct enough. Mary Jane said on an impulse. 'Come in—I was just going to have coffee. Will you have a cup with me?'

She was bound to admit, at the end of ten minutes, that he must be a genuine cousin. After all, her grandfather had told her often enough that the nephew in Canada had a son—this would be he; he knew too much about the family to be anything else. And when he produced some letters written by her grandfather to his own father, there could be no further doubt. True, he didn't give them to her to read, but he showed her the address and the signature at the end, explaining. 'Great-uncle was very fond of my grandfather, you know—he was always making plans to visit him. He never did, of course, but he had a real affection for him—Dad was always talking about him too. Have you still got Major?'

Her last misgivings left her. She said with cautious friendliness:

'Yes—he's eleven, though, and getting a bit slow. He's in the kitchen with Mrs Body. Would you like to stay to lunch? Are you passing through or staying somewhere here?'

He accepted the invitation with an open pleasure which won her over completely. 'I'm touring around, having a look at all the places the old man told me about. I'm staying at Keswick and very comfortable.'

'Did you bring your car?' She corrected herself. 'No, of course you couldn't if you flew.'

'I've rented one.' And when he added nothing further she suggested that they should walk down to the lake. Their stroll was an unqualified success, partly because Mary Jane, who wasn't used to men— younger men, at any rate—taking any notice of her, found that not only did her companion listen to her when she spoke, but implied in his replies that she was worth listening to as well, and the glances he gave her along with the replies gave her the pleasant feeling that perhaps she wasn't quite as plain a girl as she had believed. It was a pity, she reflected, while the young man waxed enthusiastic over the scenery, that Fabian wasn't with them so that he could see for himself that not everyone shared his opinion of her. The horrid word tiresome flashed through her mind; it was amazing how it still rankled. A vivid picture of his face—austere, faintly mocking and hand-some—floated before her mind's eye. She dismissed it and turned to answer Mervyn Pettigrew's eager questions about the house and its history.

She told him all she knew, studying him anew as she did so. He had good looks, she conceded, spoiled a little by the eyes and a mouth too small—and perhaps his chin lacked determination, although, as she quickly reminded herself, after several weeks of Fabian's resolute features, she was probably unfairly influenced, but these were small faults in an otherwise pleasing countenance. She judged him to be twenty-five or six, thick-set for his height and age. His clothes were right—country tweeds and well-polished shoes. On the whole she was prepared to reverse her first hasty impression of him, and admit that he might be rather nice. It was certainly pleasant to have someone of her own age to talk to; over lunch he told her about his home in Canada, volunteering the information that he was an executive in a vast business complex somewhere near Winnipeg, that he was a bachelor and lived in the house where he had been born—an oldish, comfortable house, by all accounts, with plenty of ground around it. He rode each day, he told her, getting up early so that he could take some exercise before breakfast and going to the office. 'Do you ride?' he wanted to know.

Mary Jane frowned. 'Yes. I haven't a mount, thought. I—I've a guardian who wouldn't allow me to choose a horse for myself, otherwise I would have had one days ago.'

Her cousin looked sympathetic. 'Don't think I'm interfering,' he begged her, 'but why not tell me about it? Perhaps there's some way…surely he can't stop you…' He waved a hand. 'This is all yours, isn't it? and I suppose Great-uncle left you enough to live on in plenty of comfort, and you're over twenty-one.' He added hastily, 'At least, I suppose you are.'

He was very well informed, she thought vaguely; he knew so much. 'I'm twenty-two.' She hesitated; the temptation to confide in someone was very great, and he was family. 'It's a little complicated,' she went on, and proceeded to tell him a little about Fabian and the conditions of her grandfather's will. She was strictly fair about Fabian. He was, she supposed, a good guardian and quite to be trusted with her money, she didn't want her companion to be in any doubt about that, and she was careful not to go into any details about her inheritance—indeed, when she had finished she wasn't sure if she should have mentioned it at all, but Mervyn had seemed very sympathetic and she was further reassured by his brief, vague reply before he changed the subject completely.

He left soon after that and when she asked him if he would like to come again, agreed that he would. 'But not for a few days,' he told her. 'I have some business to do, in Carlisle—friends I promised to look up for someone back home, but I'll call and see you again when I get back.'

She watched him go with some regret; he had helped to pass the day, it had been pleasant to talk to someone and have company for lunch. She went along to the kitchen where Mrs Body was sitting in the shabby, comfortable armchair she had used ever since Mary Jane could remember, and asked that lady what she thought of their visitor.

'He seems nice enough,' said Mrs Body, 'very friendly too. Is he coming again?'

'He said he would.' Mary Jane picked up one of the jam tarts the housekeeper had put to cool on the kitchen table and ate it.

'You'll get fat,' declared Mrs Body, 'picking and stealing between meals. Where's he from?'

Mary Jane ate another tart and told her.

'Why did he come?'

Mary Jane explained that too and then asked a little worriedly, 'Don't you like him, Mrs Body?'

'I've no reason to dislike him, but I don't know him, do I? I'm not quick to take a fancy to anyone.'

'You liked Mr van der Blocq...'

'That's different. Now if you take Major for a quick walk, I'll have tea ready by the time you get back.'

'Let's have it here,' begged Mary Jane, and went off obediently with the dog.

Mervyn didn't came for five days, during which time Mary Jane thought of him quite a lot while she busied herself about the house and the garden, writing letters to her friends at Pope's and answering a long dramatic letter from Cousin Emma, who, it seemed, had quite recovered from her father's death and was engaged in refurbishing her wardrobe—several pages were devoted to the outfits she had bought and intended to buy, to the exclusion of all other news. Fabian wasn't mentioned, nor had he written. That he was a busy man, Mary Jane was well aware, but he could surely have telephoned? But that took time, especially if he needed every free minute he had in order to take pretty girls out…she was aware that she was being unfair to him, but he could have taken some notice. When she wrote her Christmas cards, she sent him one too, and although sorely tempted to put a note in with it, she didn't do so.

She was in the kitchen helping Mrs Body and Lily with the Christmas puddings when Mervyn arrived. He apologised for disturbing her, offered her a box of chocolates with disarming diffidence and invited her out to lunch. 'There's a place in Cockermouth,' he told her, 'where we could eat, and I wondered if you would help me choose one or two things to take home with me—presents, you know.'

She felt faint dismay. 'You're not going back to Canada before Christmas?'

'I haven't any reason for staying longer.'

'What a pity! I was going to invite you to spend Christmas Day here.'

He didn't answer at once and he had turned his head away as he replied:

'That's a sufficiently good reason for me to cancel my flight, Mary Jane.' He turned and gave her a long, steady look. 'I've thought of you a good deal. When I came to England I decided to come and look you up, because you were family—but now I keep thinking of all kinds of excuses to keep me here.'

Mary Jane listened to him, enchanted. No one—no young man, that was—had ever talked like that to her before. All of a sudden she felt beautiful, sought after, and dripping with charm; it was a pleasant sensation. She smiled widely at him and said a little breathlessly, 'Well, don't go until after Christmas—it's only ten days.' They stared at each other in silence and then she said, 'I'll go and put on my coat—there's a fire in the sitting room, I won't be a minute.'

It was the first of several such expeditions. They would return after their shopping and have tea, and then, later, dinner, to return to the sitting room fire and talk until Mervyn got up to go about ten o'clock. He was an amusing talker, preferring to tell her about his own life than ask her questions about her own, although sometimes she would find that, almost without knowing it, she was answering questions she had hardly noticed about the house and its contents and whether she had enough to run it properly and if her capital was in safe hands. She told him about Mr North, assuring him that he had been the family solicitor for years and was very much to be depended upon.

'Oh, is that the North who lives in Keswick?' he asked carelessly.

'Is there one in Keswick? No, Carlisle—Lowther Street. The firm's been there for ever.'

He had made no comment and had gone on to talk about something else.

He got up to go soon after and she walked with him to the door. As he put on his coat he said, 'I've some business to see to in the morning—a call to

Winnipeg. May I come after lunch and take you out
to tea?'

She nodded happily and he kissed her lightly on
the cheek as she opened the door. It took her a long
while to go to sleep that night; it was a pity that her
excited thoughts of Mervyn were interlarded with un-
solicited ones of Fabian.

She felt a little shy when he arrived the next afternoon, but it seemed that he felt no such thing; he
kissed her again, a good deal more thoroughly this
time, and told her gaily to get her coat and drove her
into Keswick, where they had tea, bought a few things
Mrs Body had need of, and drove home again. It was
dark already, although it was barely four o'clock, for
the mountains had swallowed up what light there had
been, only the water of the lake gave back a dim
reflection. It would be cold later on, but they didn't
care. They roasted chestnuts by a blazing fire and ate
their dinner together, and after Mervyn had gone, with
yet another kiss, Mary Jane had skipped into the
kitchen, her plain face alight. Mrs Body looked up as
she went in, asked Lily to take some more logs to the
sitting room and when she had gone, observed,
'You're happy, Miss Mary Jane.' Her kind eyes were
sharp. 'Has he proposed?'

Mary Jane flung her arms round Mrs Body's ample
waist. 'Oh, Mrs Body, do you think he's going to?
No one has ever proposed to me before.'

'Which is no good reason for accepting him,' counselled her companion shrewdly.

Mary Jane knitted her fine pale brows. Mrs Body's

remark was a sensible one, but it didn't fit in with her own reckless mood. 'Oh, I know that,' she declared gaily, 'but we get on so well and he's such a dear—you know, thoughtful and interested in the house and careful of me—making sure that my future's secure and all the rest of it.' She laughed. 'He actually wanted me to take out an insurance policy!'

Mrs Body said quickly, 'You didn't take any notice of that?'

'Well, I couldn't even if I'd wanted to, Mr van der Blocq sees to all that, but I didn't bother to tell Mervyn... What shall I give him for Christmas?'

Mrs Body made one or two uninspired suggestions, adding, 'And that nice Doctor van der Blocq, what are you sending him?'

'Why, nothing,' said Mary Jane. 'He's got everything in the world, you know.' She danced off again to take Major for his bedtime trot around the garden.

It was several days later, when they were out walking on the hills, heavily wrapped against the cold, that Mervyn let fall that he had met someone who had a roan for sale, sixteen hands, with plenty of spirit but good-tempered with it. 'I know you promised this guardian of yours not to buy a horse, but if you gave me an open cheque, I could buy it for you. I'm not a bad judge and I dare say I could strike a good bargain.'

Mary Jane paused on the slope they were working their way down. 'Well, I'm not sure—I should love it, but Fabian did say that I wasn't to buy one...'

'Yes, but don't you think that he said that because

he wasn't here to give you his advice? Probably he was afraid that you might be tricked out of your money—you know how unscrupulous some people are—but surely if I picked out a good mount for you, he wouldn't raise any objection?'

Put like that, it had a ring of reasonableness. Besides, Fabian probably wouldn't come again for months—she would never get a horse of her own. She said thoughtfully: 'All right, I'll give you a cheque. Will you see to it for me, please? I'm sure Fabian won't mind.'

The words sounded curiously false in her own ears, Fabian would mind. He would mind on principle, because he was her guardian and considered that she shouldn't do anything at all without first asking his permission. Indignation swelled her bosom and gave way to a feeling of sneaking relief because he wouldn't know anyway.

The horse arrived two days later, a nice beast who went to his stable quietly enough, although he had a rolling eye. Mervyn explained that the animal was little nervous but would settle down in a day or so. He told her what he had paid for him too, a price which rather shocked her, but when she ventured: 'Isn't that rather a lot?' she was met with a chilly surprise.

'I had to haggle to get him at that price, but if you could have done better...' He left the rest of the sentence in mid-air, where it hung between them like a small, disturbing cloud. It evaporated during the day, but she made a mental note that Mervyn was touchy about money and she would have to remember that.

It was Christmas Eve the following day, and Mervyn had said that he wouldn't be out until the afternoon, but he had kissed her warmly as he had said it and she hadn't really minded because she had planned to go riding—just a short canter across the fields by the lake, to see how Prince went. The morning was bright and clear and still very cold as she saddled him and led him out of the stable. He was still nervous, dancing along beside her, shying at every stone, and although she wasn't nervous herself, she could see that she would have to go carefully; he was a great deal more spirited than Mervyn had led her to believe. Perhaps in Canada they were used to horses that bucked and shied at every blade of grass. She had him away from the house by now, walking him across the meadow towards the water, she coaxed him to a standstill with some difficulty and was preparing to mount when Fabian spoke very quietly somewhere behind her.

'Don't, Mary Jane, I beg of you.' He was beside her now and had taken the reins into his own hands while she stared up at him speechlessly, a little pale in the face and with a most peculiar tumult of feeling inside her. He was pale too, but all he said was: 'He's not the horse for you—I told you to wait until I could find you something suitable. You broke your promise...'

'I didn't,' she said quickly, 'Mervyn bought him.' She missed the sudden fire in his dark eyes. 'Mervyn?' repeated Fabian softly. 'Let us go back to the house and you shall tell me about—er—Mervyn!'

He began to lead Prince back to his stable and she perforce, walked with him and waited while he saw to the animal, and then accompanied him into the house to find Mrs Body, beaming with delight, hurrying with coffee and some of her mince pies.

'I knew you would come, Doctor dear,' she told him happily, 'with Christmas tomorrow.' She put down the tray and went to the door. 'I've the nicest piece of beef in the oven ready for your lunch.'

She went out of the room and Mary Jane said with polite haste, 'I hope you'll stay to lunch.' She busied herself with pouring coffee and didn't look at him. His clipped 'thank you' sounded coldly on her ears.

After a lengthening silence during which she sought for and discarded a number of conversational openings, Fabian said, 'And now if you would be good enough to explain about this horse.' He spoke in tones which brooked no hindrance; she explained at some length and in a muddled fashion which in the end left her with no alternative but to tell him about Mervyn too. He heard her out, no expression upon his calm, handsome features, and saying nothing, so that when she had finished she was forced to ask: 'Well?'

He raised his eyebrows. 'My dear Mary Jane, what am I expected to say? I haven't met this cousin yet, although I shall be delighted to do so, even if only to point out to him that I find his taste in horseflesh a little on the inexperienced side.'

Her gentle eyes flashed. 'Pooh! You only say that because you didn't pick Prince yourself.'

He ignored this. 'And what did you pay for him?'

She was a truthful girl, so she told him, waiting for his expected comment on the excessive price, but he said nothing, staring at her with narrowed eyes. Presently he said, 'Not a local animal, I fancy.' He sounded so casual that she let out a sigh of relief. 'No, Mervyn told me he had heard of him from someone he knew in Keswick.'

'Is that all you know?' She sensed the mockery in his voice and bristled as he continued, 'Surely you have the receipt and the bill of sale?'

'Mervyn will let me have them,' she protested, feeling guilty because she hadn't given the matter a thought. 'How is your cousin?'

If she had hoped to change the conversation she was unlucky. 'Very well, thank you. And when is Mervyn coming to see you again?'

She muttered, 'This afternoon,' and fidgeted under his look.

'Excellent. I shall enjoy meeting him. Had you planned anything? I shan't be inconveniencing you in any way?' His cold politeness chilled her. He got up. 'By the way, Prince has a slight limp in his left hind leg—you will agree with me that it should be attended to at once? I know it's Christmas Eve, but I'll see what I can do.'

He went out of the room, leaving Mary Jane with her mouth open in surprise. She hadn't noticed any limp, though now that she came to think about it,

Prince had stumbled once or twice. She wouldn't be riding for a day or two; it might be a good idea to get it looked at.

Fabian came back presently and she asked, 'Did you find a vet?'

He strolled over to the window and stood half turned away from her, looking out on to the wintry morning. He said at length, 'Yes—he'll see what he can do some time today.'

'It's not serious?'

He turned to look at her across the pleasant room. 'No, but I don't think you should ride him, though. Now tell me, how are you managing? Have you sufficient money?'

They spent the remainder of the morning in a businesslike fashion, and over lunch they kept to common places while she wondered silently why he was so abstracted in his manner. Once or twice she found him staring at her in an odd fashion, with an expression which she couldn't understand, and indeed, he was so unlike his usual cool, arrogant self that she began to feel quite uncomfortable. And asking questions hadn't helped either, for she had tried that with singularly little success, in fact he had remarked after one such probe into what he had been doing: 'I have never known you take such an interest in my life— should I feel flattered?'

She felt as uncomfortable as she knew she looked. 'No, of course not, but I haven't seen you for several weeks. I just wanted to—to hear what you've been doing.'

His eyes held a gleam in their depths. 'Then I am flattered. Tell me, what are your plans for Christmas?'

'Well, nothing much. Mervyn's coming for Christmas Day—after church, you know, and I expect he'll stay until after dinner, and on Boxing Day some of Grandfather's friends are coming for a drink. Mervyn will be coming to lunch again, but he says he can't stay to meet Doctor Morris, he's got some people to see. It's a pity, because Doctor Morris knew his father, I believe.'

Fabian leaned back in his chair. 'A great pity,' he commented in a dry voice. 'It sounds very pleasant.'

'And you?' she asked politely, and then struck by a sudden thought, added in tones of the utmost apprehension, 'You're not staying for Christmas, are you?'

Somehow the thought of Mervyn and Fabian together filled her with an uneasiness she knew was quite unjustified; she closed her eyes on the vivid picture her mind had conjured up of Fabian blighting Mervyn's cheerful talk with his damping politeness.

His companion's face remained unaltered in its blandness. 'I wasn't aware that I had been asked. Set your mind at ease, Mary Jane, I shall be leaving within an hour or so.'

'Oh well, that's all right,' she exclaimed, so relieved that she hardly realised what she had said. 'Do you mind sitting here while I see if lunch is ready? There's some sherry on the window table, do help yourself.'

She went out of the room, humming cheerfully. If

Fabian was going so soon, he and Mervyn would only have to meet for a very short time, perhaps not at all.

Her optimism was ill-founded. They had barely finished Mrs Body's excellent lunch when Mervyn drove up, parked the car in front of the door, and walked in. To say that he was surprised was too mild a way of putting it—Fabian had put his car in the garage; there had been no hint of anyone else being in the house, so Mervyn came breezing into the sitting room, to stop short just inside the door, looking so disconcerted at the sight of Fabian lounging in a chair by the fire that he could say nothing. It was Mary Jane who plunged into speech.

'Mervyn—hullo. Fabian, this is Mervyn Pettigrew, my—my cousin from Winnipeg. Jonkheer van der Blocq, my guardian.'

Fabian had risen and advanced to meet Mervyn, saying in a suave voice which somehow disturbed Mary Jane: 'Ah, Mr Pettigrew, Mary Jane has been telling me about you. I'm glad to have this opportunity of meeting you.'

He smiled, but his eyes were cold, and before Mervyn could say anything he went on: 'You must tell me about your home—Canada is a place I have often wished to visit. Your home is in Winnipeg? In the city itself or outside?' He waved Mervyn to a chair. 'Sit down, my dear fellow, and tell me about it.'

The conversation was in his hands; Mary Jane sat helplessly listening to Mervyn answering her guardian's questions, and even when she made attempts to change the conversation, she was frustrated by Fabian's blandly polite pause while she did so, only to have him resume his remorseless cross-examination again. Quite fed up, she suggested an early cup of tea because then Fabian might remember that he was leaving shortly… She was half way to the door when she heard a car, voices and some sort of commotion; she got to the window in time to see a horse-box and a Land-Rover disappearing down the drive. Prince's head was just visible.

She cut ruthlessly into Mervyn's description of the grain harvest. 'They've taken Prince!' she uttered, and turned to look at Fabian, who returned her startled gaze with a placid unsurprised face. 'I mentioned it,' he reminded her mildly.

'Yes, I know—but I didn't know he was going. Where is he going to?'

'The vet has taken him into his stables. A very good man, I believe.'

'Prince? The horse I bought for Mary Jane?' Mervyn's voice sounded strained. 'What's wrong with him?'

'A limp—the near hind leg, my dear fellow. Nothing much, probably he did it after you saw him. A splendid animal, I must congratulate you on your choice. Which reminds me, Mary Jane couldn't remember from whom she had bought him—you have the papers on you, I daresay.'

Mervyn searched his pockets. His face was a little pale, he looked harassed. 'I've left them at the hotel,' he muttered. 'I quite intended to bring them—I must remember tomorrow.'

'Of no consequence.' Fabian's voice had a silkiness which struck unpleasantly upon Mary Jane's ears as she came back into the room. 'What did you pay?'

Mervyn answered before she had a chance to remind Fabian that she had already told him, and rather to her surprise, Fabian merely nodded his head, remarked that the price of horseflesh had risen out of all bounds, and went on to say that doubtless such a splendid beast would be well known in the district. 'I must go along and see his owner,' he observed casually, 'and see if he has anything as good. Where did you say he lived?'

Mary Jane watched the hunted look on Mervyn's face and wondered about it, and when he said at length that he couldn't exactly remember, helpfully suggested the names of some of the local breeders, to all of which Mervyn answered rather shortly that none of them was correct. At last, goaded by her excessive helpfulness, he said, 'It wasn't a breeder—just someone selling privately.'

'Ah,' Fabian's voice was still hatefully silky. 'Doubtless one of the small estates around here—I should have no difficulty in finding him.'

There was no knowing what Mervyn would have replied to this if Mrs Body hadn't come in at that minute with the tea tray. Mary Jane poured tea and oil upon what she felt might be troubled waters if she allowed the two men to go on long enough, but she need not have bothered, for Fabian seemed to have lost interest in Prince and his former owner. He was talking, much more freely than he usually did, she thought, uneasily, about the house and it contents, which, he assured Mervyn in a manner quite unlike his own somewhat reserved one, were by no means without value and likely to become more so. 'A very nice little property,' he said as he got up to go, 'worth quite a considerable sum in the market today.'

He was about to shake hands with Mary Jane when Mervyn spoke.

'I may not see you again—I hadn't intended to say anything just yet, but as you are here…I want to marry Mary Jane—I understand from her that she needs permission from you before she can marry. Well, I should like it now.'

This speech, uttered in urgent tones, had the effect of silencing Mary Jane completely, although it had no such effect upon her guardian, who remarked airily, 'My dear chap, why didn't you mention this earlier? Now I am forced to leave on most urgent business, and you can quite understand that I'm not prepared to give my consent until we have had a little talk about your prospects and so on. But I imagine that you will be here for another week or so? I'll endeavour to come and see you at the earliest opportunity.'

He glanced at Mary Jane, his face empty of expression. 'I'm sure that you both have a great deal to talk about. Goodbye, Mary Jane. I have no need to wish you a happy Christmas, have I—but I do, just the same.'

He took her hand, and she stared up into his face, completely out of her depth, filled with the ridiculous wish that he wouldn't go away, but stay for Christmas. She whispered some sort of reply and stayed in the middle of the room, watching him walk away.

Mervyn talked a lot after Fabian had gone. He talked about their future together and how he had been wanting to tell her that he loved her for several days. 'We'll get married after Christmas,' he urged her. 'There's no reason why we should wait, is there? I can move in here…'

She was surprised at that. 'But won't you have to go back to Winnipeg? What about your work? Do you want to give up your job there? and if you come here to live you'll have to get something else. Wouldn't it be better if I came to Winnipeg?'

He was adamant that that wouldn't do. 'You would be homesick,' he told her, 'and this will be a marvellous home for us both—we'll get another car, and a boat—something fast.'

She agreed happily, in a rose-coloured future, not quite real. She asked him, 'And your income? Is it enough for us to live on?'

'Oh, don't worry your little head about that,' he assured her, and kissed her. 'We'll go into all that when we're married.'

'But I don't suppose Fabian will let me get married until all that's sorted out. He takes his duties very seriously.'

Mervyn caught her hands in his. 'Look, darling, why do we wait for him? If we get married he can't do anything about it, can he? He's far too busy a man to get involved in our business—besides, he'll be glad to be rid of this guardianship—that is, unless he's feathering his own nest with your money.'

Mary Jane felt a sudden fierce rush of sheer rage. 'That's a beastly thing to say!' she said loudly. 'Fabian is the most honest man alive, he wouldn't touch a penny that wasn't his—besides, he's frightfully rich.'

Mervyn apologised at once, turning it into a joke, but the sour taste of it stayed with her for the rest of the evening, despite his gay talk, although she found it hard to resist his charm. He would be a delightful husband, she assured herself, and how lucky she was that he had appeared out of the blue to fall in love with her and want to marry her. She wished him a warm good night, all her small qualms forgotten, and went along to find Mrs Body making last-minute preparations for the following day while Lily stood at the sink cleaning the vegetables. Mary Jane drew up a chair to the table and began to blanch a bowl of almonds standing on it.

'He's gone,' said Mrs Body sadly.

'Just this minute, but he'll be back for lunch tomorrow.'

Mrs Body thumped the stuffing she was making with quite unnecessary vigour. 'Not him,' she sounded aggrieved, 'Doctor van der Blocq, and I'd like to know where he's going to spend his Christmas.'

Mary Jane, her mouth full of almonds, said indistinctly, 'Holland, I suppose.'

The housekeeper gave her an impatient look. 'Now, Miss Mary Jane, you know as well as I do that he can't get back all that way by tomorrow morning—not with the car, he can't. What are you about not to think of that? It fair bothered me to see him driving off alone this afternoon—didn't you give him a thought?'

'Yes—no—I had something else to think about. Mrs Body, darling Mrs Body, I'm going to be married!'

'To that Mr Pettigrew? Well, I suppose it was to be expected, though how he could allow you to ride that wild animal I can't think. I never was so pleased to see the animal go again—he should have known better. Good thing dear Doctor van der Blocq came along like he did.'

'Oh, Mrs Body, aren't you pleased?' Mary Jane sounded as forlorn as she suddenly felt. 'I thought you would be—I'm not going to be an old maid after all.'

Mrs Body rallied. 'Of course I'm pleased, my dear, there's nothing I'd like better than to see you wed. But Canada's a long way off.'

Mary Jane reached over the table and kissed her housekeeper and friend on the cheek. 'But I'm not going there—Mervyn suggested that he should move in here just as soon as we're married.'

'And Doctor van der Blocq—does he know?'

'Oh yes, Mervyn told him this afternoon, and Fabian said he'd come back very shortly and they'd have a talk—about money and things.' She got up. 'I'm going to get something to drink—we'll toast Christmas before we go to bed.'

She went to sleep almost at once, thinking about the perfect future she was going to have with Mervyn, but she didn't dream of him, she dreamed of Fabian, driving his car endlessly through a lonely Christmas. She remembered it when she wakened in the morning and it became real somehow when Mrs Body brought her early tea and laid a small package on the bed.

'A Happy Christmas, Miss Mary Jane,' she said, 'and the dear doctor asked me to be sure and give you this first thing in the morning.'

There was a velvet box inside the wrapping paper, and in the box was a brooch, a true lovers' knot in rose diamonds, exquisitely beautiful. Mary Jane stared at it for a long time because it somehow seemed to be part and parcel of her dreams, its sparkle, a little blurred because of the sudden tears in her eyes, tears because she hadn't given him anything at all—she hadn't even invited him for Christmas. She remembered with shame that she had let him see her relief when he had told her that he was going away again. He must have said that because he was too proud a man to say anything else. She wondered forlornly where he had gone.

CHAPTER SIX

DOWNSTAIRS, Mary Jane found a delicately painted porcelain bowl on the breakfast table, filled with a gorgeous medley of tulips, hyacinths and dwarf iris. She sniffed their perfume delightedly and looked for a card. They would be from Mervyn, of course. She wandered into the kitchen to wish the others the compliments of the season, exclaiming: 'Those heavenly flowers—I wonder where he got them this time of year?'

Mrs Body dished bacon and eggs before replying. 'Brought them all the way from Holland, he did—made me promise to look after them and put them on the table first thing in the morning. It's a lovely bowl—ever so old. He gave us presents too, but we haven't opened them yet.'

Mary Jane remembered her remorse before she had gone to sleep, and it came crowding back into her head now—even if the flowers and the brooch had only been a gesture from a guardian to his ward, they had been gifts, and she had been horribly unkind. Once more she wondered where he had gone and if he had expected to stay. She pushed the thought away and with it the faint regret that the flowers hadn't been Mervyn, even the brooch, although possibly he couldn't have afforded that. It struck her anew that he had never talked about money to her at all, only sketched in a vague background, leaving her to suppose that he was comfortably off. She sighed, for she was a romantic girl and had always cherished the idea that a man in love went to any lengths to please his girl-friend, and yet it had been Fabian, not Mervyn who was so in love with her, who had taken care that there would be presents waiting for her when she got up on Christmas morning. She ate her breakfast thoughtfully and then went, with Mrs Body and Lily, to church. Mrs Body and Lily wore the new leather gloves Fabian had given them, and Mary Jane wore the brooch.

They had a drink when they got back and then got the lunch ready together. Mrs Body and Lily had friends to share theirs, so Mary Jane laid the table in the dining room for herself and Mervyn. By the time he arrived she was feeling gay and lighthearted, having spent a good deal of the morning persuading herself that Fabian had only called in on his way to somewhere and wouldn't have stayed even if she had asked him.

She had bought Mervyn a picture, a landscape by a local artist of some repute. She gave it to him when he arrived and watched while he unwrapped it, admired it and then laid it on the table in the window. There was an awkward pause until he said, 'I had no idea what to get you—we'll go together and find something later on.'

She made excuses for him—perhaps in Canada they didn't set much store by Christmas—but surely he could have brought a few flowers? She wasn't a greedy girl, only hurt because she had expected that because he loved her, he would have wanted to express that love with some small gift. She stifled the hurt and smiled at him. 'That will be nice,' she agreed. 'And now what about a drink before lunch?'

The bowl of flowers was on the table; he couldn't help but see it. He commented idly upon it, remarking that it looked a valuable piece.

'I don't know about that,' she said uncertainly. 'Fabian sent it.'

He frowned. 'Now that we're going to be married,' he stated categorically, 'I'm not sure that I like you receiving valuable gifts from him, even if he is your guardian.'

She flushed a little and said with a spurt of temper, 'Why ever not? As you said, he is my guardian, and what harm is there in giving a girl flowers? We do it a lot in England—for birthdays and Christmas.'

It was his turn to get angry. 'I don't like it,' he reiterated stubbornly. 'Before you know where you are he'll be giving you something really valuable— jewellery—bought with your money, no doubt.'

'I hope you'll apologize for that.' Mary Jane's voice was quiet, but it shook a little. 'I thought I had made it plain to you that Fabian wouldn't touch a penny of my money—he's my guardian, not a thief,' she added defiantly. 'He gave me this brooch.'

Mervyn stared at it across the table. Presently he said sullenly:

'Oh, all right, I'm sorry I said it—I didn't mean it,

you have to make allowances for a man being jealous when he's in love.' His eyes were still glued to the brooch. 'It looks very expensive—I thought it was something you had inherited from your grandfather.'

He smiled at her. 'I'm a brute behaving like this on Christmas Day, darling. I'm sorry—I suppose I'm a bit on edge. I want to marry you, you see, as soon as possible, and I can't think of anything else but that. I promise I'll make it up to you when we're married.'

He was charming for the rest of the day; she basked in his admiration and listened happily to the delightful things he said, knowing right at the back of her mind that most of them were grossly exaggerated if not completely untrue. No one had ever told her before that she was pretty, nor had they spared more than one glance upon her eyes, which Mervyn declared were quite remarkably lovely; her common sense, buried in a haze of wishful thinking, told her that. But no one had ever been in love with her before, she had no yardstick by which to measure him. She allowed herself to believe every word and squashed her common sense, almost squashing her resolve to wait for Fabian's permission before they married. It was tempting, especially when Mervyn showed her the special licence he had bought, sure that she would give in when she saw it. But she still refused and put his sulky silence down to disappointment on his part.

During the following few days he had become a little difficult, and once or twice, when she was alone and quiet, a small voice deep inside her wanted to know if she really loved him or was she just being

swept off her feet because she had never been in love
or loved before. She buried the thought under a host
of more pleasant ones and scoffed at her doubts.

But they stayed; she asked Mrs Body about them,
and that dear soul looked troubled even while she
spoke reassuringly. 'And wait until the dear doctor
comes,' she counselled. 'It can't be long now.'

It was Old Year's Day when Fabian came. Mary
Jane had expected Mervyn to lunch; she had spent
most of the morning helping Mrs Body in the kitchen
because Lily had gone home for the day and now she
sat at the desk in one of the sitting room windows,
writing thank-you letters, and keeping an eye on the
drive and the road beyond. It had turned cold once
more, there were a few snowflakes falling and the
frost had been heavy the night before. She had put on
a new dress, a dark green pinafore with a matching
crêpe blouse under it, and had pinned the diamond
brooch into it. She had done her hair with more patience than usual too, but it was getting a little untidy
again, for she had a habit of running her hand through
it while she was writing and it was two hours since
she had done it. She was shocked when she saw the
time; it was past one o'clock—something must have
delayed Mervyn, and she couldn't think what. She
resolved to wait another half an hour and applied herself to her letters again, but only for a few minutes,
for a car turned into the drive and she got to her feet
and ran to the door without bothering to look out of
the window.

It was the Rolls, and Fabian who got out of it. He

came in slowly, looking tired, and the sight of his shadowed face stirred a desire deep inside her to help him. But Fabian wasn't a man to accept help or admit tiredness, so she said instead, 'Hullo, how nice to see you, and just in time for lunch—it's a bit late, because I'm expecting Mervyn. You'll be able to talk to him.'

'We have had our talk, and he won't be coming.'

He stood in the open doorway, towering over her, his face expressionless, staring down at her, making no effort to move or take off his coat.

Mary Jane gave him a puzzled look. 'Why isn't he coming? He particularly wanted to see you—he's got a special licence.' She bit her lip and went on in a cold little voice, 'Where did you see him?'

'In Keswick.' He paused. 'I have to talk to you, Mary Jane.'

'He's ill—hurt? Oh, Fabian, do tell me quickly!'

'It's neither. If we could go somewhere?'

'Yes, of course, and you must have something, you look tired to death.'

He smiled grimly. 'When I have finished what I have to say and you still want me to remain perhaps you will ask me then.' He sounded suddenly impatient. 'The sitting room?'

He didn't sit down, but walked over to the window and then turned to face her. 'Mervyn isn't coming. He won't be coming again. He has left Keswick and is already on his way to catch his plane, back to Canada.'

She felt the blood leave her cheeks. 'I don't believe you—he loves me.'

'I wouldn't lie to you, Mary Jane. He was no good, my dear girl—you are such an innocent.' He sighed. 'Oh, he was your cousin all right, always borrowing money from your grandfather, like his father before him, an undischarged bankrupt with not a penny to his name, who came to hear of your grandfather's death and saw a chance of easy money. And how much easier could it have been?' His voice took on a mocking, angry note. 'You, a little bored already, with a house of your own and money—quite a lot of money...'

She interrupted him, almost stammering. 'He had no idea—I never told him.'

'No? But he tricked old Mr North into telling him how much the estate was worth. I suppose you told him where North lived?' And when she nodded miserably: 'I thought so. And Prince—how could you have been so feather-witted, Mary Jane? Did you not wonder why he never showed you the papers connected with the sale, or the receipt? Why, I smelled a rat the moment you said—or were you so infatuated with him that you couldn't be sensible any more? Do you know what he paid for Prince? Exactly half the amount he told you. He had the rest; he hired a car in your name too—I paid the bill just now, and the hotel—he owed several weeks' bills and told them that you would pay.' He thrust an impatient hand into a pocket and tossed some papers at her. 'There, see for yourself.'

She left them to drift to the floor. 'How—how did

you find out all this?' She tried to speak in a normal voice, but it came out in a miserable whisper.

'I asked around—it wasn't difficult—and then I flew to Winnipeg and made some enquiries.'

'You went to all that trouble?' She had her voice nicely under control now, but the effort to hold back the tears was getting beyond her. She said in a sudden burst: 'Did it matter? He's the only man who has ever asked me to marry him, do you know that? He said he loved me and now you've spoiled it all—I believe you want me to go on living here for ever and ever— I hate you, I hate you, I wish I'd never set eyes on you!' She hiccoughed and choked, then took a breath, for she had by no means finished. Her heart, she most truly believed at that moment, was broken, and nothing mattered any more. All she wanted to do was to hurt the man standing so silently before her; his very quiet made her feelings all the hotter. But the words tumbling off her tongue were stilled by the entrance of Mrs Body with a loaded tray, who after one sharp glance at Mary Jane addressed herself to Fabian.

'I saw the car, Doctor dear, and I said to myself, "He'll be cold and hungry, I'll be bound," so here's coffee and sandwiches, and a Happy New Year to you.' She poured the coffee. 'And where did you spend Christmas, if I might ask?'

'Oh, in Keswick, Mrs Body. I had business there.'

'But why didn't you stay here? If Miss Mary Jane had known...'

'That had been my hope.' He smiled at her with great charm, and Mrs Body, quite overcome, exclaimed, 'You mean to say you came for Christmas and we never even gave you a good Christmas dinner?'

'It didn't matter. As it turned out I had a good deal to do. Thank you for the coffee.'

'Well, you look as though you need it, and no mistake, Doctor dear—worn out, you are. Have you come from Holland?'

He shook his head. 'Canada.'

Mrs Body was no fool. She said, 'Lor' bless my soul! I always knew…' She shot another look at Mary Jane, standing like a statue, taking no part in the conversation, and went out of the room, shutting the door very gently.

Fabian had made no attempt to drink his coffee, and when Mary Jane turned her back upon him he watched her for a few moments and then said softly: 'Mary Jane,' and when she didn't answer: 'I'm sorry, but I had to do it. I couldn't see you throw yourself away on a wastrel and ruin your whole life.' He paused. 'Do you want me to stay?'

She didn't turn round, only shook her head. She heard him cross the room and then the hall, and presently the front door was opened and shut again, and the Rolls murmured its way down the drive. By straining her ears Mary Jane could hear it going down the road, back to Keswick and, she guessed miserably, Holland. He wouldn't come again. There was no need to hold the tears back any longer; she flopped into the nearest chair and cried her eyes out, and when Mrs Body came back, sobbed out the whole sorry story to her, to be comforted and scolded a little and comforted again. 'And that poor man,' said Mrs Body, 'gone again without a bite to eat inside him, and him such a great man.'

'He can starve!' said Mary Jane savagely into Mrs Body's ample bosom.

'Now, now, dearie, that's no way to talk. I never said so, but I didn't fancy you marrying that Mr Pettigrew—far too glib, I found him. I know your heart's broken, but it'll mend, my dear, and you'll think differently later on, and when Mr Right pops the question you'll have forgotten all this.'

'But there isn't a Mr Right!' wailed Mary Jane.

'I'm not so sure about that,' said Mrs Body bracingly, and smiled to herself over the tousled brown head on her shoulder.

But despite Mrs Body's comforting words, Mary Jane found the days which followed hard to live through; she walked herself into a state of exhaustion, going over and over in her mind all that had happened, forcing herself to face the truth—that Mervyn hadn't loved her at all, only her money and her home, seeing her as an easy way to live in comfort for the rest of his life. Just as Fabian had said. She told herself that she would get over it, just as Mrs Body had told her, but in the meantime she was utterly miserable, not least of all because Mervyn hadn't written. He could have at least wished her goodbye—but then she hadn't said goodbye to Fabian either, had she? She had let him walk out of the house, cold and tired and hungry; even if she hated him—and of course she did—she had been pretty mean herself.

By the end of the week she wasn't eating much, nor was she sleeping; her mood was ripe for the letter from Pope's which arrived after a particularly bad night. It was from Miss Shepherd, telling her that there was a severe 'flu epidemic in London, the hospital was halfstaffed and overflowing with patients, and how did Mary Jane feel like helping out on a temporary basis for a week or so?

Mary Jane went straight to the telephone, packed a bag, hugged Mrs Body and Lily goodbye and got into the Mini. She would only be gone for a week or so, but the prospect of having some hard work before her was just what she needed. She drove down the motorway, still unhappy, it was true, but finding life bearable once more.

It was amazing to her that she could slip back into life at Pope's with such ease, and still more amazing that it should be Women's Surgical to which she was sent, because the regular staff nurse was herself down with 'flu. Mary Jane went on duty a few hours after her arrival to find Sister Thompson sitting in her office, drumming impatient fingers on the desk while she harangued a part-time staff nurse whom she obviously didn't like; she didn't like Mary Jane either, but at least they knew each other, a fact she pointed out somewhat acidly before giving her a dozen and one things to do. Mary Jane, impervious to her bad temper, and relieved to have so much on her hands that she had no time to think, went into the ward, to be greeted happily by several nurses she had known. The ward was heavy and full with beds down the centre and cases going to theatre, to return requiring expert care and nursing. Sister Thompson sailed up and down between the beds, giving orders to anyone who was within earshot, complaining bitterly that there were no good nurses any more, and what was the world coming to—a purely rhetorical question which none of her harassed staff had neither the time nor the inclination to answer, at least not out loud.

Mary Jane, worn out after her hard day, slept as she hadn't slept for nights, and what was more, ate her breakfast the next morning. Despite her hard work, a faint colour had crept into her white face and the hollows under her eyes, while still there, weren't quite so noticeable. She was off duty in the afternoon, the day was cold and grey and the staff nurses' sitting room in the Home looked bleak—there were several of her friends off duty too, so she rounded them up and they went in a cheerful bunch to Fortnum and Mason's where they had tea before embarking on a quick inspection of the January sales. She went back to the ward refreshed, and because Sister Thompson was off duty that evening, the work went better than it usually did. She went off duty that evening with the pleasant feeling that at least she had done a good day's work and slept soundly in consequence.

The days slid by, each one packed with work and the small petty annoyances which went with it. Mary Jane found little time to think of anything but drips, pre-meds, closed drainage and the preparation of emergency cases for theatre, and at night she fell into bed and was asleep before she had time to shed one single tear over her broken romance with Mervyn. Just once or twice, when she was in theatre with a patient, she was reminded of Fabian, because the operating theatre was his world; it surprised her that in place of the rage which had possessed her against him, there was now only a dull feeling, almost a numbness. Beneath the mass of bewildered thoughts and memories she had expected him to write to her despite the manner of his going, but nothing came, only letters from Mrs Body, detailing carefully the day-to-day life at home. She had hoped for a letter from Mervyn too, against all her better judgement, but as the days went by and she realised that he wasn't going to write, she knew that that was the best thing. He had never loved her, and she had been a fool to have imagined he did. He would never have left in that craven fashion if he had had even a spark of feeling for her, and certainly nothing Fabian could have said would have deterred him from at least explaining to her. She sighed; it was a pity she didn't like Fabian, for quite obviously he had done his best for her, though in an arrogant fashion and with a total disregard of her feelings for which she would never forgive him.

With each day she found that she was recovering slowly. It was no good moaning over the past, and she had much to be thankful for; a home, enough money, kind Mrs Body and the willing Lily. She would go back to them soon and pick up the threads of her life where Fabian had so ruthlessly broken them off. She would have to find something to do, of course; Red Cross, part-time nursing, something of that sort. And she could sail and ride—only she hadn't a horse, and unless Fabian came to see her again, she was unlikely to have one. Perhaps she would have to wait until she was thirty and free to do as she wished. Her thoughts were interrupted by Sister Thompson's sour voice, enquiring of her if she intended to be all day making up that operation bed and how about Mrs Daw's pre-med? And Mary Jane, who had already given it, said 'Yes, Sister,' in a mechanical way and went to see how the last case back from theatre was doing.

Op days were always extra busy. Sister Thompson went off duty after lunch and the atmosphere of the ward brightened perceptively even though an emergency appendix was admitted, followed by a severely lacerated hand. Mary Jane slogged up and down the ward, a little untidy now but still cheerful though a thought tired. She was going out that evening with some of her friends; there was a film which was supposed to be marvellous, but the way she felt by teatime, she didn't really care if she saw it or not, though probably once she was there she would enjoy it, and anything was better than sitting and thinking.

She was almost through giving the report to Sister Thompson before she went off duty when she was interrupted by the telephone. Sister Thompson lifted a pompous hand for silence and addressed the instrument with her usual severity, although this softened

slightly when she discovered that the speaker was
Miss Shepherd. She put down the receiver with a
strong air of disapproval, observed: 'Matron'—she
still called Miss Shepherd Matron because she didn't
agree with all the new-fangled titles everyone had
been given by the Salmon Scheme—'Matron,' she repeated, 'wishes to see you in her office as soon as
possible. First, however, you will finish the report.'

Mary Jane, luckily at the tail end of her recital,
made short work of the rest of it, wished her superior
good night, waved to such of the patients who were
in a fit state to notice, and started off down the corridors and staircases which separated her from Miss
Shepherd's office. The hospital was fairly quiet except for the distant clatter of dishes denoting the ad-
vent of patients' suppers. She met no one and paused
only long enough to fling open the door of Men's
Medical where one of her friends worked, acquaint
that young lady with the tidings that she might be late
and they had better go on without her, and then tear
on once more. The office was at the end of a short
passage. Mary Jane knocked on the door, watched the
red light above it turn to green, and went in.

Miss Shepherd was sitting at her desk and Fabian
was standing in the middle of the room with his hands
in his pockets, contemplating a very bad portrait of
the first governor of Pope's. He took his eyes from
it, however, as Mary Jane entered and met her startled
gaze. She went red and then white, opened her mouth
to speak, clamped it shut and turned for the door,

quite forgetful of Miss Shepherd. It was that lady's calm voice which recalled her to her senses.

'Ah, there you are, Staff Nurse. Your guardian is most anxious to speak to you,' she smiled across the room at him as she spoke. 'I'm sure you will want to hear what he has to say.'

'No,' said Mary Jane baldly, 'I wouldn't.' She looked at Fabian. 'Why should you want to see me? I can't imagine any good reason...' She stopped because he was looking at her so oddly, and Miss Shepherd said smoothly:

'All the same, I think you might like a little talk.' She got up and went to the door and Fabian opened it for her with a smile. 'I have a short round to make, ten minutes or so. I daresay that will be long enough.'

She had gone. Fabian leaned against the door, watching Mary Jane, who, very conscious of his gaze, stared in her turn at the portrait on the wall.

'I had no intention of seeing you for some time,' Fabian began coolly, 'this is purely to oblige Cousin Emma. I did a thyroidectomy on her a week ago— she is doing very well, but now she insists that she won't return home unless you are there to look after her. I telephoned you, of course, but Mrs Body, although she knew you were here, had no idea how long you would be staying. Miss Shepherd tells me that she can let you go immediately.'

'There are plenty of nurses in Holland,' said Mary Jane flatly, while she thought with sudden longing of the old house in Midwoude and even more longingly of Fabian's great house by the canal. 'I don't want to go,' she added for good measure.

He chose to ignore this. 'Emma likes you—more, she has an affection for you, she feels that she will never make a complete recovery unless you are there to help her. And it is important that she recovers completely, for Trouw has asked her to marry him and although she longs to do so, she says that she will refuse him unless she is quite well again. And I think that you are the one to convince her.'

Womanlike, Mary Jane had fastened on the piece of news which aroused her interest most. 'Married? How marvellous! Oh, I am glad, and of course she must marry Doctor Trouw. I always thought...she must be very happy.'

Her voice died away because she herself should have been feeling very happy too, married by now, surely—instead of which, she was standing here in Miss Shepherd's office listening to Fabian's calm demands on her time and energy. She said in a husky little voice, à propos of nothing at all:

'I haven't a horse—what happened to Prince?'

Fabian made a sudden movement and then was still again. 'I know. Prince is now owned by the vet. I believe he's very content and they suit each other very well.' He began to walk towards her. 'Mary Jane, I told you that I had no intention of coming to see you, for I am only too well aware of your feelings towards me—you made them abundantly clear—but I am fond of Cousin Emma and I want her to be happy; she has spent a great deal of her life looking after Uncle Georgius—very inadequately, I must admit, but she did her best. And now happiness is within her reach and unless we help her, her stubbornness is likely to ruin everything.' His voice roughened. 'And you need entertain no fears that I shall be under your feet. When I come to see Cousin Emma it will be as her surgeon, not as your guardian. In future any meetings we may have shall be strictly on a business footing, I promise you that.'

For some unaccountable reason her heart sank at his words, for despite his indifference towards her, she had come reluctantly to regard him as someone to whom she could turn. She knew now, standing so close to him in the austere little room, that she had always been aware of him somewhere in the background, ready to help her if she needed help, and despite their dislike of each other he never had and never would let her down.

She was horrified to find her eyes filling with tears. They spilled down her cheeks and she wiped them away quickly, miserably aware that she looked quite hideous when she wept. But she was too proud to turn her face away. 'I'll come because Cousin Emma wants me,' she told him, 'not because you asked me.'

'I hardly expected that.' His voice was remote, as was his expression. They stared at each other in silence for a few seconds and Mary Jane, watching his calm face felt a keen urge to talk to him, to tell him how she felt. She blew her nose and wiped away the last tear and would have embarked on heaven knew what kind of speech, only she was interrupted by the return of Miss Shepherd, who sat down at her desk and asked pleasantly, 'Well, all settled, I hope?'

'Indeed yes, Miss Shepherd. You did say that my ward could leave immediately?'

'Of course. We are very grateful to the girls who came back to help us, but we wouldn't dream of keeping them a moment longer than necessary—Staff Nurse Pettigrew would have been going in a day or two, in any case.'

'Splendid!' He turned to Mary Jane. 'I'll send your tickets to the front lodge, shall I? Could you be ready to leave tomorrow evening?'

She was surprised. She had taken it for granted that she would be with him; that he would take her back to Holland. She was on the point of saying so and prevented herself from doing so just in time, for of course he would have no wish for her company and she had no wish for his. Her voice was as cool as his own had been. 'Yes, I can.'

'You have enough money?'

'Yes.'

There was a little pause until Miss Shepherd said briskly, 'Well, that seems to be settled, doesn't it? I won't keep you, Staff Nurse—you are off duty, I believe.'

Mary Jane said that yes, she was. She thanked Miss Shepherd, said goodbye in a cold voice to Fabian and went through the door he was holding open for her. It shut behind her, a fact which disappointed her; she had half expected him to follow her out. She even loitered down the corridor, so that, if he wished, he

would have ample time to catch her up. He did no
such thing, so rather put out, she went off to the
Home.

Her friends had gone, leaving a note saying that
they would wait outside the cinema until seven
o'clock and after that it would be just too bad. Her
watch said twenty minutes to the hour; to bath,
change, catch a bus to Leicester Square and arrive at
seven o'clock was an impossibility. She would spend
the evening writing to Mrs Body and packing her few
things. She tore off her cap and flung it on the bed,
flung off her apron and belt too and was about to give
her uniform dress the same rough treatment when
there was a knock on the door.

'Oh, come in,' she called crossly, ripping pins out
of her hair, and turned to see Fabian standing in the
doorway. She forgot that they were barely on speaking terms, that she hated him, that he was arrogant
and always had his own way. 'For heaven's sake,'
she breathed, 'you can't be here! This is the Nurses'
Home—it's private...' She waved an agitated hand at
him. 'Men don't come upstairs—there's a little room
by the front door...'

'For boy-friends?' he wanted to know. 'But I'm not
a boy-friend, Mary Jane.' He sounded serious, but she
could have sworn that he was laughing. 'There was
no one downstairs, you see, so I looked in the War-
der's office and found your room number.'

'You've got a nerve!' she told him fiercely, still
whispering. 'Go away!'

'Of course, if you'll have dinner with me.'

She tossed a curtain of honey-brown hair over her shoulders. 'No, I won't,' she said tersely, then gasped as he came in. 'Supposing the Warden comes along?' she begged him. 'Do go—I'll get into trouble and—and you'll lose your reputation.'

She gave a small shriek at the great roar of laughter he gave. 'Oh, please, Fabian,' she said, quite humbly.

He went to the door at once. 'Half an hour,' he told her. 'I'll be in the—er—boy-friends' room, and don't try and give me the slip. Possibly you will find the situation easier if I assure you that I'm not asking you out for any other reason than that of expediency. I'm leaving England in a few hours and I should like to tell you about Emma before I go, it will be easier for you when you arrive.'

She joined him in half an hour exactly, wearing new clothes she had bought for herself because she had wanted to look nice for Mervyn—a burgundy red coat with its matching dress, a red velvet cap on her pale brown hair, expensive gloves and handbag and suede boots with leather cuffs. She was thankful that she had found time to pack them when she left home to go to Pope's, for she had nothing much else with her—a skirt, a handful of sweaters and her sheepskin jacket which she had flung into the back of the Mini.

They dined at a nearby restaurant, and it wasn't until he had ordered and they were sipping their drinks that he abandoned the polite, meaningless conversation with which he had engaged her during their drive from Pope's. She had answered him in monosyllables, fighting a feeling of security and content, induced, she had no doubt, by the comfort of the Rolls and the anticipation of a delicious meal.

'You are sure that you have enough money?' he wanted to know again.

She mentioned the amount she had and he raised his eyebrows in surprise. 'My dear girl, you will be with Emma for at least two weeks, that's barely enough to keep you in tights.'

'How do you know I wear tights?' she demanded.

His lips twitched. 'I don't live in a monastery. I'll see that there's some money with your ticket. You had better travel to the Hoek by the night boat from Harwich. Someone will meet you there and drive you up to Midwoude. Emma is still in hospital, I should like you to be there when she is fetched home—that will be arranged. You'll need some overalls or something similar for a few days. What size are you?'

'Twelve,' she told him. She had no idea that he was such a practical man.

He eyed her thoughtfully. 'Twelve what?' His voice was bland.

'Well, that's my size—the number of inches I am.'

'Vital statistics?' and she saw the twinkle in his eyes and said severely: 'Yes.'

He made a note. 'Must I guess?' he asked mildly. 'Thirty-four, twenty-two, thirty-five or six—inches, of course. Is that near enough?' and when she nodded, speechless, he went on pleasantly: 'Now, as to Emma—I did a sub-total on her. She has needed it for a year or more, but she always refused—you know how thyroidtoxicosis cases refuse treatment. Besides,

I think she felt that she would be letting Uncle Georgius down in some way, but now the way seemed clear for an operation; it was Trouw who persuaded her. It is all very successful, but she doesn't believe it yet—I think you will be of great help in convincing her. Besides, you can encourage her to make plans for her wedding.' He stopped, staring at her, his eyes hooded and she felt her cheeks go white.

'That was unpardonable of me, Mary Jane, I'm sorry.' He looked away from her strained face and continued in an impersonal voice, 'She has made a satisfactory recovery—a sore throat and hoarseness, of course. She's on digitalin and Lugol's iodine, and there are several more days to go with her antibiotic.' He added, 'She's a terrible patient. If you decide to change your mind, I shall quite understand.'

'I haven't changed my mind.'

'I didn't think you would.' He smiled at her and beckoned the waiter. 'The chocolate gateau is delicious here, would you care to try it?'

They were halfway through it before he spoke again. 'Mary Jane, you shall have your horse. I'll go over to the Lakes as soon as I can spare the time and find a good mount for you.' He shot her a lightning glance. 'You need not worry, I won't expect an invitation to stay.'

She didn't look at him. 'That sounds like a bribe.'

She wished she hadn't said it, for he at once became remote and haughty and faintly impatient. 'Don't talk nonsense,' he told her sharply. 'And now if you will listen carefully, I will finish telling you about Emma's treatment.'

The rest of the evening was businesslike in the extreme, for the talk was of such a professional nature that they might have been on a ward round at Pope's. He took her back without loss of time after dinner and wished her goodbye at the hospital gate with the air of a man who had concluded a satisfactory deal and now wanted to forget about it for pleasanter things.

'He's so unpredictable,' said Mary Jane, talking to herself as she went through the hospital to the Home, and a harassed night nurse hurrying in the opposite direction flung over her shoulder, 'They all are, ducky.'

Mary Jane left the following evening, her ticket and more money than she could possibly spend safely in her handbag, what clothes she had stowed in her case. She had wished Sister Thompson goodbye and had been told, to her surprise, that she was no worse than all the other girls who thought they were staff nurses, and if she chose to return at any future date, she, Sister Thompson, would personally ask Miss Shepherd if she could be posted to Women's Surgical ward. Mary Jane, overwhelmed by this treat for the future, thanked her nicely, took a brief farewell of such of her friends as were about and climbed into her taxi, reflecting that even if life wasn't treating her as kindly as it might, at least she had no time to sit and repine. When the friendly taxi-driver asked her if she was going on holiday she told him, 'Work,' adding to puzzle him, 'Work is the great cure of all the maladies and miseries that ever beset mankind.'

He grinned at her. 'Have it your own way, miss.'

CHAPTER SEVEN

IT WAS Doctor Trouw who met the boat at the Hoek van Holland, and Mary Jane, a little wan after a rough crossing, was delighted to see him, although the delight was tinged with disappointment—probably she told herself bracingly as she responded to the doctor's friendly greeting, because she was tired and for some reason, lonely. She would feel better when she reached Midwoude, where she had no doubt her days would be filled.

Doctor Trouw had a Citroën, large and beautifully kept. She sat beside him responding suitably to his pleased speculation upon his hoped-for marriage to Cousin Emma. 'We have always been fond of each other,' he told her gruffly, 'and now that my wife is dead...' He paused. 'I feel that life still has much to offer.' He coughed. 'Of course, we are neither of us in the first flush of youth.'

'I don't see that that matters at all,' said Mary Jane with sincerity. 'There's not much point in getting married unless you're sure that you're going to be happy, and that could happen at any age. I'd rather wait for years and be certain.'

Her companion looked pleased and plunged into plans for the future; she suspected that he was really thinking aloud for the pure pleasure of it—which left her free to consider what she had just said. If she had married Mervyn would he have been the right man? Unbidden, the thought that she hadn't liked him when she had first seen him crossed her mind, to be instantly dismissed—he might have treated her badly, but that was no reason for her feelings to change, or was it? If she had loved him, surely her feelings wouldn't have changed. What did she feel for him now, anyway? Dislike—indifference? She wasn't sure any more, she wasn't even sure now that she had ever loved him. It was all very bewildering and a relief when Doctor Trouw stopped for coffee.

They reached Midwoude just before noon, to be welcomed by Jaap, and Doctor Trouw didn't wait—he had some cases to see, he explained, but he would be back at two o'clock, if she could manage in the meantime.

She and Jaap managed very well, each speaking their own language and understanding the other very well in spite of it. She had the same room as she had had previously and he took her case up for her, telling her that lunch would be in half an hour and leaving her to unpack, do her face and tidy her hair. She did this slowly, savouring the peace and quiet and comfort around her. After that afternoon, when Cousin Emma was home again, she wouldn't be quite so free, so she might as well make the most of her leisure now.

The hospital at Groningen was large and imposing with a medical school attached. Doctor Trouw skirted the main building, and halfway down a side turning

ran the car under a stone archway and into an inner
courtyard, where he parked the car. Mary Jane, getting out, guessed it to be the sanctum of the senior
staff of the hospital and knew she was right when she
saw the Rolls in a far corner. They entered the hospital through a small door which led to a short dark
passage which spilled into a wide corridor with splendid doors lining its walls, and scented with the faint
unmistakable smell of hospital cleanliness. It was also
very quiet. The consultants would gather someone behind these richly sombre walls, as would the hospital
board, and VIPs visiting the hospital would, no doubt
drink their coffee, cocooned in its hushed affluence.
All hospitals are alike, Mary Jane decided, treating
carefully in Doctor Trouw's wake.

He opened a door almost at the end of the corridor
and gave her a kindly prod. The room was large, it's
centre taken up by an oblong table hedged in by a
symposium of straight-backed chairs. There were
other chairs in the room, easy ones, grouped round
small tables, and the air was thick with cigar smoke.
It seemed to her that the room was full of men—large,
well-groomed men, every single one of whom turned
to look at her. In actual fact there were a bare dozen,
senior members of the hospital medical staff who had
just risen after a meeting.

'Over in the far corner,' said Doctor Trouw in her
ear, and began to steer her to where Fabian was standing. He had his back to them, talking to two other
men, but he turned and saw them and came to meet
them. He looked, thought Mary Jane a trifle wildly,

exactly what he was; a highly successful surgeon with plenty of money, plenty of brains and so much self-confidence that he could afford to look as though he had neither. She felt depressed and a little shy of him, for he seemed a stranger, and her reply to his pleasant 'Hullo, Mary Jane' was stiff and brief. But he seemed not to notice that; enquiring after her journey, whether she had slept and if she felt herself capable of under-taking the care of Emma within the hour. She told him yes, checking an impulse to address him as sir, and with a perception which took her by surprise he remarked:

'We all look rather—er—stuffy, I suspect. What-ever you do, don't address me as sir.'

She smiled at that. 'Not stuffy,' she assured him. 'It's just that you all look so exactly like consultants, and so many of you together is a bit overpowering.'

The two men laughed as they ushered her to the door again, pausing on the way to introduce her to various gentlemen who would have gone on talking for some time if Fabian hadn't reminded them that they were expected elsewhere. They traversed the cor-ridor once more, this time to a lift. It was a small lift, and with Doctor Trouw's bulk beside her and Fabian taking up what space there remained, she felt some-what crowded, and more so, for the two men carried on a conversation above her head, only ceasing as the lift purred to a halt, to smile down at her for all the world as though they had just remembered that she was there.

They stepped out into another wide corridor, this

time lighted from the windows running its whole length and lined on one side by doors, each numbered, each with its red warning light above the glass peephole in its centre. They entered the first of these to find Cousin Emma sitting in a chair, dressed and waiting, and if Mary Jane had been in any doubt as to Fabian's sincerity when he had told her how much his cousin needed her, it could now be squashed. Cousin Emma uttered a welcoming cry, enfolded her against a fur-clad, scented bosom and began a eulogy upon Mary Jane's virtues which caused her face to go very red indeed.

'I knew you would come!' breathed Emma. 'I said to Fabian, "If Mary Jane doesn't come, I shall make no effort to recover from this dreadful operation."' She paused, allowed Mary Jane to assume the upright and swept aside her mink coat.

'The scar,' she invited dramatically. 'Look at the scar—is it not dreadful? How can a maimed woman accept an offer of marriage with such a blemish?'

Mary Jane considered the hair-fine red line drawn so exactly across the base of her patient's throat. 'You won't be able to see it in three months' time,' she pronounced. 'Even now it's hard to see unless one stares—and who's going to stare? All you need to do is to get a handful of necklaces which will fit over it exactly—we'll do that, one for each outfit.'

She smiled at Cousin Emma, her eyes kind, unheedful of the two men standing close by.

'I feel better already,' declaimed Emma, and smiled

with all the graciousness of some famous film star. 'I'm ready.'

Fabian drove her back in the Rolls and Mary Jane followed behind with Doctor Trouw in the Citroën, giving all the right answers to her companion's happy soliloquising. He would be, she considered, exactly right for Cousin Emma, for he obviously worshipped the ground she trod upon, while being under no illusion regarding her tendency to dramatise every situation. She asked: 'When do you hope to get married, Doctor Trouw?'

'Well, there is no reason why we shouldn't marry within a week or so. All the preliminaries are attended to—I persuaded her to become *ondertrouwt* before she went into hospital. Perhaps you could persuade her?' He looked at her hopefully. 'She is a sensitive woman,' he explained, just as though Mary Jane wasn't already aware of it, 'and prone to a good deal of dejection. Once we are married, I believed that can be cured.'

He turned the car in through the open gates and pulled up beside the Rolls. 'Willem is home,' he told Mary Jane as they got out. 'I daresay he will be over one day to see you.'

'How nice,' said Mary Jane, not meaning it—she foresaw a busy time ahead, acting as confidante to father and son while each confided their romantic problems to her. She sighed soundlessly and followed him into the house.

She had said almost nothing to Fabian, nor he to her, nor did he attempt to speak to her before he left very shortly afterwards. He had told her, she recalled, that he would be his cousin's surgeon when he called and not her guardian, now it seemed he had every intention of keeping his word. She answered his brief nod as he went with something of a pang and went to make Cousin Emma comfortable.

It proved an easier task than she had supposed. For one thing the operation had been a success; in place of the emotional, overwrought woman she had been, Cousin Emma had become quieter; her feverish gaiety and sudden outbursts of tears had been most effectively banished. She was still rather tearful, but that was post-operative weakness and would disappear with time. In the meanwhile, Mary Jane kept her company, saw to her pills and tablets, cared for her tenderly, talked clothes, reassured her at least twice a day that the scar was almost invisible, and coaxed her to eat her meals. And when Fabian came, as he did each day, she met him with a politely friendly face, answered his questions with the right amount of professional exactitude, commented upon the weather, which was bitterly cold once more, listened carefully to any instructions he chose to give her, and then retired to a corner of the room, to resume her knitting. Only when he got up to go did she put it down— thankfully, as it happened, because she wasn't all that good at it, and walk to the door with him and see him out of the house. It was on the fifth day after her arrival that he paused on the steps and turned round to face her.

'Have you recovered?' he wanted to know coolly.

'Though perhaps I'm foolish to ask such a question, for you're not likely to tell me, are you?'

'No, I'm not,' she replied in an outraged voice, her eyes no higher than his waistcoat. She spoilt this by adding: 'It's not your business, anyway.'

He grinned. 'Who said it was? Willem Trouw was asking about you yesterday. He doesn't know about your broken romance and he's having difficulties with his own love life. I believe you might console each other.'

Mary Jane was furious, so furious that for a moment the words she wanted to say couldn't be said. At last: 'You're abominable—how dare you say such things? You're cruel and heartless!' She tried to shut the door in his face, but he took it from her and held it open.

'Probably I am,' he agreed, 'but only when I consider it necessary.' He bent suddenly and before she could turn her head, kissed her mouth. Then he shut the door gently in her surprised face.

Willem came over that very afternoon, and remembering Fabian's words, she was hard put to it to be civil to him; supposing Fabian had said the same sort of thing to Willem? Perhaps men didn't confide in each other, but to be on the safe side she refused Willem's invitation to go out with him that evening, doing it so nicely that he could always ask again if he wanted to.

She had been there more than a week when Fabian, on one of his daily visits, mentioned casually that the continuous frost had made it possible to skate on the lake. 'Do you skate?' he wanted to know.

They were in the little sitting room, Cousin Emma in an easy chair, leafing through a pile of fashion magazines, Mary Jane determinedly knitting. She bent her head over it now, rather crossly picking up the stitches she had dropped, and became even crosser when Fabian remarked:

'I think you are not a good knitter, for you are always unpicking or dropping stitches or tangling your wool.'

He was right, of course; she had been working away at the same few inches for days, for the pattern always came wrong. Probably she would tear it off the needles and jump on it one day. Now she left the dropped stitches and knitted the rest of the row, briskly and quite wrongly, just to let him see how mistaken he was. It was a pity that he laughed.

'There are skates in the attic,' Cousin Emma informed anyone who cared to listen. 'I shall not skate, naturally, but you, Mary Jane, must do so if you wish. It is a splendid exercise and Willem could come over and teach you if you aren't good at it.' She added complacently, 'I'm very good, myself.' She glanced at her cousin. 'What do you think, Fabian?'

Mary Jane wasn't sure how it happened. All she knew was that within minutes she had agreed—or had she?—to spend the following afternoon skating with Willem. It would be so convenient, said Emma, because Doctor Trouw was coming over to discuss wedding plans with her, and Willem could come with him. They would stay to tea, of course, and Mary Jane might like to make that delicious cake they had had a few days ago—Cook wouldn't mind.

Mary Jane replied suitably, doggedly knitting. But in the hall she said to Fabian: 'I don't particularly wish to skate with Willem, and I should be much obliged if you would mind your own business when it comes to my free time...'

He put on his car coat and caught up his gloves. 'My dear girl, have I annoyed you?' His voice was bland, he was smiling a little. 'Perhaps you have other plans—other young men you prefer to skate with?'

He was still smiling, but his eyes were curiously intent.

'Don't be ridiculous, you know I haven't.' She went on gruffly: 'When can I go home? Emma is almost well.'

He was pulling on his gloves and didn't look at her. 'No one would wish to keep you here against your will, Mary Jane, but I think that Emma would be broken-hearted if you should wish to go home before her wedding.'

'Will they marry soon?'

'I imagine so. Are you homesick?'

She raised puzzled eyes to his. 'No—at least, I don't think so. I—I don't know. I feel unsettled.'

He put a compelling finger under her chin. 'Unhappy?' His voice was gentle. And when she shook her head, 'The truth is that you are still in a mist of dreams, are you not? But they will go, and you will find that reality is a great deal better.'

He went away and she stood in the lobby watching the Rolls being expertly driven down the frozen drive and away down the road. Sometimes he was so nice, she thought wistfully, wondering what exactly he had meant.

She went skating with Willem when he came because there was nothing she could do about it—he arrived with his father, his plans laid for an afternoon on the ice with her. He had even borrowed some skates, and despite everything, she enjoyed herself. The lake was crowded, the bright colours of the children's anoraks lent the scene colour under the grey sky, their shrill, excited voices sounding clearly on the thin winter air. Willem was a good skater, if unspectacular. They went up and down sedately while he told her about the girl he wanted to marry and who didn't seem to want to marry him. 'I can't think why,' he told her unhappily. 'We're such good friends.'

'Sweep her off her feet,' advised Mary Jane. 'I don't know much about it, but I think girls like that. You could try—you know what I mean, be a bit bossy.'

'But I couldn't—she's so sure of what she wants, at least she seems to be.'

Mary Jane executed a rather clumsy turn. 'There, you see? Probably she doesn't know her own mind. Where is she now?'

They were going down the length of the lake again. 'As a matter of fact she's in Groningen.'

'Today? This afternoon?' Mary Jane came to such an abrupt halt that she almost lost her balance. 'What could be better? Go and fetch her here, make her put on skates and rush up and down with her until she's worn out—show her who's master.' She gave him a push. 'Go on, Willem—she'll be thrilled!'

'You think so?' He sounded undecided and she re-iterated: 'Oh, go on, do!'

'But what about you?'

'I'm all right here. If I'm not back by dark you can come and fetch me.'

'Really? You don't think I'm being—being not friendly towards you, Mary Jane?'

'No, Willem. It's because we're friends that we can make this plan.' She started off, waving gaily. 'Have fun!'

She didn't look round, but when she turned and came back, he had gone.

The afternoon darkened early and became colder, but she, skating with more enthusiasm than skill, glowed with warmth; she had on her sheepskin jacket and a scarf tied tightly over her bun of hair, and she had stuffed her slacks into a pair of Cousin Emma's boots—they were too big, but they did well enough, as did the thick knitted mitts Jaap had found for her. Her ordinary little face was pink with pleasure and exercise, her eyes sparkled; that she was alone didn't matter at all, because there were so many people around her, enjoying themselves too. She skated to the end of the lake and then, the wind behind her, came belting back. There were fewer people now; the children were leaving, and there was more room. She was almost at the end when she saw Fabian some way ahead, right in her path. Even in the gathering dusk there was no mistaking his tall, solid figure. She began to slow down, for, most annoyingly, he hadn't moved. She was still going quite fast when she reached him, but he stayed where he was, putting out a large arm to bring her to a standstill.

'Whoops!' said Mary Jane, breathless. 'I thought I was going to knock you over—you should have moved.'

He was still holding her. 'No need. I weigh fifteen stone or thereabouts, and I doubt if you're much more than eight.' He laughed down at her. 'You show a fine turn of speed, though I don't think much of your style.'

'Oh, style—I enjoy myself.'

He had turned her round and they were skating, hands linked, back down the lake. Presently he asked, 'Where is Willem?'

'He's gone to Groningen to meet his girl-friend.'

'I thought he was spending the afternoon with you?'

'Oh, we started off together, then he started telling me about her and really, he was so fainthearted, I thought I'd better encourage him to go after her.'

'So you gave him some advice?'

'That's right. Have you the afternoon off?'

'More or less, but I must go home shortly. Will you come and have tea with me? Willem is presumably occupied with his girl, and Cousin Emma and Trouw will be engrossed with each other. That leaves us.'

She considered. 'Well, tea would be nice—but won't they wonder where I am?'

'I'll let them know. Shall we race to the end—you can have twenty yards' start.'

She did her best, but he overtook her halfway there, and then dropped back to skate beside her until they reached the bank, where they took off their skates and walked through the bare trees to where he had parked the car.

His house was warm and inviting, just as she had remembered it. They had tea in a small, cosily furnished room with a bright fire burning and lamps casting a soft glow over the well-polished tables which held them. And the tea was delicious—anchovy toast, sandwiches and miniature cream puffs. Mary Jane, with a healthy appetite from her skating, ate with the pleasure of a hungry child. She was halfway through the sandwiches when she exclaimed, 'We haven't telephoned Midwoude—do you think we should?'

Fabian got up at once. 'I suppose I can't persuade you to stay to dinner?'

She refused at once very nicely and was at once sorry that she had done so, because she would very much have liked to spend the evening with him. She told herself urgently that it was foolish to be charmed by him just because he was being such good company—besides, there was Mervyn. She pulled herself up with the reflection that there wasn't Mervyn; she owed nothing to him, neither loyalty to his memory or anything else; not, said her heart, even love, for it hadn't been love, only a plain girl's reaction to being admired...

'You're looking very thoughtful,' remarked Fabian and sat down again. 'You said you wanted to go home—will you agree to stay until Emma is married as I asked you? I think the wedding will be very soon, probably we shall hear something when we go back presently.'

She spoke at random to fill the silence between them: 'This is a lovely house.'

'You like it? It needs a family—children—in it. You like children, Mary Jane?'

'Yes.' She was unconsciously wistful as they lapsed into silence once more. She had abandoned her confused thinking, and it seemed a good thing; she needed peace and quiet to sort herself out, and Fabian's presence had the effect of confusing her still further. She wasn't even sure what she wanted any more—only one thing was clear, he didn't mind if she returned home; she had watched his face when she had told him that she wanted to go and its expression hadn't changed at all. Not meaning to say it, she asked: 'When I go home, will you need to visit me again?'

His casual, 'Oh, I think not; everything is arranged very satisfactorily. If you should need my services you can always write or telephone,' daunted her, but she tried again.

'But what about the horse?'

'I asked the vet to keep an eye open—he'll let me know when he finds something worth while.'

She said, 'Oh, how nice,' in a small forlorn voice, aware that she had been using the horse as a line of communication, as it were, and Fabian had cut the line. She got to her feet. 'I think I should be getting back,' and when he got to his feet with unflattering speed, 'You said we wouldn't meet—that you would only be Emma's surgeon—I forgot that this afternoon. Did you?'

His dark eyes rested briefly on hers. 'No, I hadn't forgotten, Mary Jane, but there is such a thing as a truce, is there not?'

He fetched her outdoor things and they went out to the car. A good thing, she thought savagely as she got in, that she hadn't accepted his invitation to dinner—uttered out of politeness, no doubt, for he was obviously longing to be rid of her. Telling herself that it didn't matter in the least, she kept up a steady flow of chat as he drove her back to Midwoude, her voice a little high and brittle.

But he seemed in no hurry to be rid of her company or anyone else's when they reached the house. Cousin Emma and Doctor Trouw were in the sitting room, the tea things still spread around them, deep in wedding plans. They would be married, declared Emma, with a suitable touch of the dramatic, in four days' time—the *burgermeester* of Midwoude had promised to perform the ceremony in the early afternoon at the Gemeentehuis, and afterwards they would cross the street for a short ceremony in church. 'And you will come, Mary Jane, because you have been so kind and

good...' the ready tears sprang to her eyes, 'and when
you marry I shall come to your wedding.'

'How nice,' said Mary Jane briefly. 'Tell me, what
will you wear?'

Her companion was instantly diverted and the two
ladies became absorbed in the bridal outfit. They were
still engrossed in this interesting topic when the gentlemen wandered off to the other side of the room to
have a drink, and when after a few minutes Fabian
said that he must go, he did no more than pass a
careless remark about their pleasant afternoon before
he took himself off.

There was no time for anything but the wedding
preparations during the next day or so. Cousin Emma,
fully recovered from her operation, plunged into a
maelstrom of activity with Mary Jane doing her best
to hold her back a little. Recovered she might be and
in the happy position of having others to attend to her
every want, she still needed to rest. Mary Jane gently
bullied her on to the chaise-longue in her bedroom
each afternoon and by dint of guile and cunning, kept
her there until Doctor Trouw called at tea-time. Fabian came too, but only for a few minutes, to check
his cousin's progress, although on the day previous
to the wedding he remained long enough to tell Mary
Jane that should she wish, he would arrange for her
to travel home on the day after the wedding. 'But time
enough to let me know,' he assured her carelessly.
'There are few people travelling at this time of year,
it will only be a question of a few telephone calls.'

He had nodded cheerfully at her and added, 'I shall see you at the wedding, no doubt.'

Getting Cousin Emma to the Gemeentehuis proved a nerve-shattering business. Not only was she excited and happy, she was tearful too, and when almost dressed declared that she looked a complete guy, that her shoes pinched and that her scar was so conspicuous that she really hadn't the courage to go through with the ceremony. It was fortunate that her bridegroom—come, as Dutch custom dictated, to fetch his bride to their wedding—had brought with him his wedding gift, a string of pearls which exactly covered the offending blemish. Mary Jane, rather pink and excited herself, left them thankfully together and hurried to the front door. Jaap was to drive her to the village and she was already a little late. He wasn't there, but Fabian was, strolling up and down the hall in morning clothes whose elegance quite dazzled her.

'There you are,' he remarked. 'I sent Jaap on, you're coming with me.' He stood looking at her. 'Now that is a new hat,' he decided, 'and a very pretty one.'

Mary Jane gave him a doubtful look. The hat had taken a good deal of thought and she hadn't had all that time to escape from Cousin Emma. It matched her coat exactly, a melusine with a sideways-tilted brim ending in a frou-frou of chiffon. Not at all her sort of hat, but after all, it was a wedding and one was allowed some licence. It added elegance to her ordinary face too and gave it a glow which almost amounted to prettiness.

'Someone told you,' she accused him.

'No, indeed not,' he laughed at her, 'and it really is pretty.'

She wished that he would say that she was pretty too, although that would be nonsense, but he didn't say anything else, but tucked her into the Rolls beside him and drove off to the Gemeentehuis, a small, very old building, ringed around now with a number of cars and little groups of people from the village. Inside, Fabian found her a seat at the back before he went to take his place with his family in the front row. The ceremony was short and quite incomprehensible to her, but the service in the church was more to her taste, for she was able to follow it easily. And when it was over she watched the bride and groom and their families, correctly paired, walk down the aisle to the door of the church. She knew none of them, save for Fabian and Willem. They looked, she considered, a little haughty, very well dressed and faintly awe-inspiring, although the younger members of the party were gay and smiling and enjoying themselves. Willem, she was glad to see, had his girl with him—at least, she hoped it was his girl. He certainly looked happy enough, and Fabian—Fabian was escorting a truly formidable lady of advanced years, just behind the bridal pair.

She waited until almost everyone had gone and made her way to the door, looking for Jaap. He was nowhere to be seen. There were still several groups of people lingering around the porch, but they were all strangers to her. She supposed she would have to walk. She frowned—how like Fabian to forget all about her; she wished she hadn't come, he was horrible, thoughtless, thoroughly beastly... He touched her arm, smiling at her, so that she felt guilty, and felt even more so when he said, 'I knew you would have the sense to wait until I came for you—Great-aunt Corina isn't to be hurried. Come on.'

She travelled back sitting with the old lady, who wasn't haughty at all, while a large young man, whom Fabian introduced as Dirk—a cousin—squeezed in beside them. Fabian introduced the girl sitting beside him too—a blue-eyed creature wrapped in furs. Her name was Monique, and even though he said she was a cousin, Mary Jane didn't take to her. She was still pondering the strength of her feelings about this when they arrived at the house.

The vast drawing room had been got ready for the reception, with a long table and a number of smaller ones grouped around it. Mary Jane, seated between Dirk and an elderly uncle of the bride, found that she was expected to make a good meal. She went from champagne cocktails to lobster meuniere, from venison steaks to chocolate profiteroles, each with its accompanying wine. It was a relief to hear from Dirk that a wedding cake wasn't customary, for what with the wine and champagne and the warmth of the room, she began to feel a little lightheaded. Even the haughty members of the family didn't seem haughty any more, indeed, those she had spoken to had been charming to her. She glanced round her. Everyone looked very happy, but then marriages were happy occasions, although if she married she would want a quiet one with just a few friends. The corners of her gentle mouth turned down; the sooner she stopped thinking that romantic nonsense, the better. She turned to Dirk, who was quite amusing although a little young, she considered, and when he asked her if he might take her out to supper that evening, she refused with a charm which drew from him a regretful smile and a promise to ask her again the very next time they met. It seemed pointless to tell him that she was going back to England the next day, she laughingly agreed and listened with all her attention while he told her about his ambition to be as good a surgeon as his cousin Fabian.

The guests began to leave as soon as the bridal pair had gone; car after car slid away into the winter darkness until there were only a very few left, their owners delaying their departure for a last-minute chat or waiting for each other. Mary Jane felt rather lost; the drawing room was in the hands of the caterers, under the sharp eye of Jaap, being returned to its usual stately perfection. Sientje was in the kitchen, the daily maid had gone long ago. Mary Jane stood in the hall, remembering how cheerfully Fabian had asked 'Tomorrow?' when she had asked him on the way to the wedding if he would arrange for her to travel home. 'I'll send the tickets here to you,' he had told her casually, 'in plenty of time for you to catch the boat train from Groningen. Jaap will drive you to the station.'

Now she wondered if that was to be his goodbye.

She had helped him when he had asked her to; her own affairs were in order, there was nothing more for him to do; did he intend to drop their uneasy acquaintance completely? Just as well, perhaps, she mused, they had never got on well. She wandered into the empty sitting room and sat down by the window, staring out into the dark evening, her mind full of useless regrets, her fingers playing with the diamond brooch Fabian had given her and which she had pinned to her coat. She had written and thanked him for it. It had been a long letter and she had tried very hard to show her gratitude, but he had never answered it, or mentioned it—she wasn't sure if he had even noticed that she was wearing it today. She got up and strolled back into the hall, empty now. Not quite empty, though, for Fabian was there, sitting in the padded porter's chair by the door. He walked over to meet her and said easily, 'Hullo—I'm just off. You're fixed up for the evening, I hear. Dirk told me earlier that he intended taking you out to supper.' He smiled. 'He's good company, you'll enjoy yourself.'

'Oh, indeed I shall,' she assured him, her voice bright. How pleased he must feel, thinking that she was settled for the evening and that he need not bother… 'I hope you have a pleasant evening too,' she assured him untruthfully, 'and thank you for seeing about the tickets. I'll say goodbye.'

She held out her hand and had it engulfed in his, and it became for an amazing few seconds of time the only tangible thing there; the hall was whirling around her head, her heart was beating itself into a frenzy because she had at that moment become aware of something—she didn't want to say goodbye to Fabian, she didn't want him to go, never again. She wanted him to stay for ever, because she was in love with him—she always had been. But why had she only just discovered it? And what was the use of knowing it now? For even as the knowledge hit her he had dropped her hand and was at the door. He went through it without looking back.

CHAPTER EIGHT

MARY JANE STOOD staring at the door for a few seconds, hoping that he might come back; that he had forgotten something; that he would ask her to go out with him that evening, Dirk or no Dirk. Anything, she cried soundlessly; a violent snowstorm which would make it impossible for him to drive away, something wrong with the Rolls, an urgent message so that she could run after him with good reason... Nothing happened, the hall was empty and silent, there was a murmur of voices from the drawing room where there was still a good deal of activity, and from outside the crunch of the Rolls' wheels on the frozen ground. They sounded remote and final; she waited until she couldn't hear them any more and then went in search of Jaap.

If the old man was surprised at her decision to go to bed immediately, he didn't show it. They had become used to each other by now, so it wasn't too difficult to let him suppose that she had a headache and wanted nothing for the night. He wished her good night and went back to the caterers.

She slept badly and got up early, which she realized later had been a silly thing to do, for the morning stretched endlessly before her. She wouldn't be leaving until the late afternoon, and somehow the time

had to be helped along. She spent some of it with
Jaap and Sientje, but conversation was difficult anyway, and they had their work to do—they were to go
on a short holiday and return to make the house ready
for Cousin Emma and her husband, who had agreed
to the happy arrangement of leaving his own house
for his son's use and carrying on his practice from
Midwoude. Mary Jane, sensing that much as Jaap and
Sientje liked her, they wanted to get on with their
chores, offered to clear away the silver and glass
which had been got out for the wedding, and then
went around freshening up the floral arrangements;
probably Jaap would throw them out before he closed
the house, but it gave her something to do. But even
these self-imposed tasks came to an end, and she ate
her lonely lunch as slowly as possible, hoping that
Fabian would telephone; surely he would say goodbye? But as the minutes ticked by she was forced to
the conclusion that he had no intention of doing so.
Perhaps he would be at the station—if she could see
him just once more before she went away... She told
herself it was foolish to build her hopes on flimsy
wishes, a good walk would do her good and she had
plenty of time. She went and got her coat, tied a scarf
over her head, snatched up her gloves, and went in
search of Jaap. He seemed a little uncertain about her
desire to go out, but she could understand but little
of what he said and she wasn't listening very hard;
she wanted to get out and walk—as fast as possible,
so that she might be too tired to think about Fabian.
She made the old man understand that she would be

back in good time for him to drive her to the station, and fled from the house before he could detain her longer.

The afternoon was bleak and frozen into stillness; the ground was of iron and she quickly discovered that it was slippery as well. She walked fast into an icy wind, down to the village, and when she looked at her watch and saw that she still had time to kill, she walked on, towards the path which led eventually to the lake. Here the bare trees gave some pretence of shelter even though the ground under her feet was rough and treacherously slithery, something she hardly noticed, trying as she was to outstrip her unhappiness, forcing herself to think only of her future in the house her grandfather had left her. She came in sight of the frozen water presently and paused to look at her watch again. She would have to return quite soon and she decided not to go any further.

There were people skating on the lake, turning the greyness of its surroundings into a gay carnival of sound and colour. Mary Jane drew a sighing breath, the memory of her afternoon with Fabian very vivid, then turned on her heel and started to retrace her steps along the path, and after a short distance, lured by the cheerful sight of a robin sitting in a thicket, turned off it and wandered a little way, absurdly anxious to get a closer view of the bird. But he flew just ahead of her so that when she finally retraced her steps the path was hidden. She hurried a little, anxious to find it again because it would never do to lose the boat train. She didn't notice the upended root under her foot—she tripped, lost her balance on the smooth ice, and fell, aware of the searing pain in the back of her head as it struck a nearby tree.

It was like coming up through layers of grey smoke; she was almost through them when she heard Fabian's voice saying 'God almighty!' and it sounded like a prayer. With a tremendous effort she opened her eyes and focused them upon him. He looked strange, for he was in his theatre gown and cap and a mask, pulled down under his chin.

'You sound as though you're praying,' she mumbled at him.

'I am,' and before she could say more: 'Don't talk.' His voice was kind and firm, she obeyed it instantly and closed her tired eyes, listening to him talking to someone close by. He had taken her hand in his and the firm, cool grip was very reassuring; she allowed the soft grey smoke to envelop her once more.

When she wakened for the second time, the room was dimly lit by a shaded lamp in whose glow a nurse was sitting, her head bowed over a book. But when Mary Jane whispered, 'Hullo there,' she came over to the bed and said in English, 'You are awake, that is good.'

Mary Jane suffered her pulse to be taken, and in a voice which wasn't as strong as she could have wished said, 'I'll get up,' and was instantly hushed by the nurse's horrified face.

'No—it is four o'clock in the morning,' she remonstrated, 'and I must immediately call the Professor—he wishes to know when you wake, you understand? Therefore you will lie still, yes?'

Mary Jane started to sit up, thought better of it because of the pain at the back of her head and said weakly, 'Yes—but no one is to get up out of his bed just to come and look at me. I'm quite all right.'

'But the Professor is not in his bed,' explained the nurse gently. 'He is here, Miss Pettigrew, in the hospital, waiting for you to wake.'

She went to the telephone as she spoke and said something quietly into it, then came back to the bed. 'He comes,' she volunteered, 'and you will please lie still.'

He was there within a few minutes, this time in slacks and a sweater. To Mary Jane's still confused eyes he looked vast and forbidding and singularly remote, and the fact disappointed her so that when she spoke it was in a somewhat pettish voice. 'You stayed up all night—there was no need. I'm perfectly all right.' She frowned because her headache was quite bad. 'It was quite unnecessary.'

He said tolerantly, 'It's of no matter,' and took her wrist between his finger and thumb, taking her pulse. 'You feel better? Well enough to talk a little and tell me what happened?'

She blinked up at him. His face looked drawn and haggard in the dim light and she felt tender pity welling up inside her so that she could hardly speak. 'I'm sorry,' she managed, 'I mean I'm sorry you've had all this trouble.'

'I said it didn't matter. What happened?' His voice

was quiet, impassive and very professional. He would expect sensible answers; she frowned in her efforts to be coherent and not waste his time.

'I went for a walk,' she explained at last. 'You see, I hadn't anything to do until it was time to leave. I went to the village and there was still lots of time—I went down the path between the trees to the lake. There was a robin, I went to look at him and I slipped and hit my head—I can remember the pain.' She stopped, thankful to have got it all out properly for him. 'I don't know how long I was there. Did I dream that I saw Jaap and it was very cold?'

Fabian had pulled up a chair to the side of the bed. 'No—you were cold, and it was Jaap who found you when he went to look for you because you hadn't gone back to the house and he was worried, only he didn't find you straight away because you were a little way from the path. You have a slight concussion—nothing serious, but you will stay here, lying quietly in bed, until I say otherwise. And you will do nothing, you understand?'

She muttered 'Um' because she was drowsy again, but she remembered to ask, 'Where's here?'

'The hospital in Groningen.' And she muttered again, 'Thank you very much,' because she was grateful to be there and wanted him to know it, but somehow her thoughts weren't easy to put into the right words. Forgetting that she had already said it once, she thanked him again. 'I'm such a nuisance and I am sorry.' A thought streaked through the fog of sleep which was engulfing her. 'I'm going home today,' she offered in a groggy voice.

'Yesterday—no, Mary Jane, you are not going home, not just yet. You will stay here until your headache has gone.'

She managed to open her heavy lids once more. 'I don't want…' she began, and met his dark eyes.

'You'll stay here,' he repeated quietly. 'Nurse will give you a drink and make you comfortable and you will go to sleep again.'

She was in no state to argue; she closed her eyes and listened to his voice as he spoke to the nurse, but he hadn't finished what he was saying before she was asleep again.

It was afternoon when next she woke, feeling almost herself, and this time there was a different nurse, a big, plump girl with a jolly face, whose English, while adequate, was peppered with peculiar grammar. She turned Mary Jane's pillow, gave her a drink of tea and went to the telephone.

Fabian was in his theatre gown again. He nodded briefly with a faint smile, took her pulse and, satisfied, said: 'Hullo, you're better. How about something to eat?'

She didn't answer him. 'You're busy in theatre,' she observed in a voice which still wasn't quite hers. 'What's the time?'

'Three o'clock in the afternoon.'

'Have you a long list?' She hadn't meant to ask, but she had to say something just to keep him there a little longer.

'Yes, but we're nearly through. How about tea and toast?'

She nodded and started to thank him, but sneezed instead. 'I've a cold,' she discovered.

'That's to be expected. The temperature was well below zero and you were half frozen. I'll see that you get something for it.'

She sneezed again and winced at the pain in her head. 'That's very kind of you,' she said meekly. 'I'm quite well excepting for a bit of a headache.'

He gave her a smile which he might have given to a child. 'I know. All the same, you will stay where you are until I say that you may get up.'

Mary Jane nodded and closed her eyes, not because she was sleepy any more, but because to look at him when she loved him so much was more than she could bear. When she opened them he had gone and the large cheerful nurse was standing by the bed with tea and toast on a tray.

It took two more days for her headache to go, and even though she felt better, the cold dragged on. Two days in which Fabian came and went, his visits brief and impersonal and kindly, during which he conferred with the nurse, made polite conversation with herself, read her notes and went away again. On the morning of the third day he was accompanied by a young man whom he introduced as his registrar, a good-looking, merry-faced young man, trying his hardest to copy his chief's every mannerism; something which might have amused Mary Jane ordinarily, but which struck her now as rather touching. He listened attentively while Fabian explained what had happened to her and agreed immediately when Fabian suggested that she might be ready to leave hospital. He stayed a little longer, talking to Mary Jane, and then at a word from Fabian, took himself off.

She had got up and dressed that morning and had been sitting by the window watching the busy court-yard below, but she turned round now to face Fabian. She had had a few minutes to pull herself together; she said in a matter-of-fact voice, 'I should like to go home tomorrow if you will allow it and it isn't too much trouble to arrange. I'm perfectly well again. Thank you for looking after me so well...'

He made a small, impatient sound. 'You will do nothing of the kind, that would be foolish, at least for the next few days. As soon as I consider you fit for travelling I will arrange your journey. In the mean-time you will come to my house—my housekeeper will look after you.'

She sat up very straight in her chair, which caused her to cough, sneeze and give herself a headache all at the same moment. Her voice was still a little thick with her cold when she spoke. 'I don't think I want to do that—it's very kind of you, but...'

'Why not?' he sounded amused.

'I've been quite enough trouble to you as it is.'

His ready agreement disconcerted her. 'Oh, indeed you have—you will be even more trouble if you don't do as I ask now. I shall be in Utrecht, and Mevrouw Hol will be delighted to have someone to fuss over while I am away. You shall go back to England when I return.'

Her reply was polite and wooden. If ever she had needed to convince herself of his indifference to her, she had the answer now. His obvious anxiety to get her off his hands even while he was treating her with such care and courtesy and arranging for her comfort, told her that, and he didn't care a rap for her...

'What are you thinking?' he demanded.

'Oh, nothing, just—just that it will be nice to be home again. Are you going to Utrecht straight away?'

He was leaning against the wall, staring at her. 'Tonight. You will be taken to my house tomorrow morning, Mevrouw Hol is expecting you. Her English is as fragmental as your Dutch; it will be good for both of you. She is a very kind woman, you will be happy with her. She has the same good qualities as your Mrs Body—to whom, by the way, I have written.'

Mary Jane was startled to think that she had quite forgotten to do that.

'Oh, I forgot—how stupid of me, I'm sorry.'

'You have had concussion,' he reminded her, and added with a little smile, 'And you have no reason to be apologetic about everything.'

She coloured painfully and just stopped herself in time from saying that she was sorry for that too. Instead she wished him a pleasant time in Utrecht, her quiet voice giving no clue to her imagination, already vividly at work on beautiful girls, dinners for two... perhaps he had another house there. He strolled to the door, his eyes on her still.

'But of course I shall,' he told her. 'I always do.' He opened the door and turned round to say, 'We shall see each other before you go, I have no doubt.' With a careless nod he was gone, and presently, by craning her neck, she was able to see him crossing the courtyard below, Klaus Vliet, his registrar, beside him. She couldn't see them very clearly because she was crying.

She left the hospital the following day, just before noon, and was driven to Fabian's house by Klaus, who called to fetch her from her room in the private wing of the hospital, explaining that his chief had told him to do so—furthermore, he was to see her safely installed with Mevrouw Hol and call daily until such time as her guardian told him not to. Mary Jane, now she was up and about, was disappointed to find that she still had a headache, it made her irritable and she would have liked to have disputed this high-handed measure on Fabian's part, but she couldn't be bothered. She accepted the news without comment and closed her eyes against the dullness of the city streets.

But inside Fabian's house it wasn't dull at all, but gay with flowers and warm and welcoming. Mevrouw Hol was a dear; round and cosy and middle-aged with kind blue eyes and a motherly face. Mary Jane, whose headache had reached splitting point, took one look at her and burst into tears, to be instantly comforted, led to a chair by the fire in the sitting room where she had tea with Fabian, divested of her outdoor things, told not to worry, and given coffee while Klaus tactfully left them to fetch her case and carry it upstairs. He joined her for coffee presently, ignoring her blotched face, and when they had finished it, ordered her to lie down the minute she had eaten the lunch Mevrouw Hol was even then bringing to her on a tray. He gave her some tablets too, with strict instructions to take them as directed. 'And mind you do,' he warned her kindly, 'or the chief will have my head.' He got up. 'I'm going now, but I shall be here tomorrow morning to see how you are. Mevrouw has instructions to telephone if you feel at all under the weather.'

Mary Jane smiled shakily at him. 'You make me feel as though I were gold bullion at the very least!'

'Better than that,' he grinned, 'above rubies.' He lifted a hand. 'Be seeing you!'

She ate her lunch under Mevrouw Hol's watchful eye and went upstairs to lie down. Her room was at the back of the house, overlooking a very small paved courtyard, set around with tubs full of Algerian irises and wintersweet. The room was delightful, not very large and most daintily furnished in the Chippendale style with *Toile de Jouy* curtains in pink and a thick white carpet underfoot. She looked round her with some interest, for it didn't seem at all the kind of room Fabian would wish for in his home. She had always imagined that above stairs, the rooms would be furnished with spartan simplicity. She didn't know why she had thought that, perhaps because he was a bachelor, but of course, the house would have been furnished years ago, for everything was old and beautiful. As she closed her eyes she thought how nice it would be to live in the old house, nicer than her grandfather's even.

She felt much better the following morning. She had done nothing for the rest of the previous day, only rested and eaten her supper under Mevrouw Hol's kindly eye and gone to bed again, and now after a long night's rest she felt quite herself again, even her headache had gone.

Perhaps it was her peaceful surroundings, she thought, as she accompanied the housekeeper on a gentle tour of the kitchen regions, for it was peaceful back in the hall she stood still, listening to the rich ticktock of the elaborate wall clock before wandering into the sitting room to sit, quite content, in one of the comfortable chairs, doing nothing. The sound of the great knocker on the front door roused her though and she got up to greet Klaus, who, after carrying out a conscientious questioning as to her state of health, joined her for coffee. He stayed for half an hour, talking gently about nothing in particular, and when he got up to go, promised to return the next day. When she assured him that this was quite unnecessary, he looked shocked and told her that he had been asked to do so by the chief and would on no account go against his wishes. Nor would he allow her to go out, not that day, at any rate.

'Well,' said Mary Jane, a little pettish, 'anyone would think that I had a subdural or a CVA or something equally horrid. I only bumped my head...'

'And caught a cold,' he told her, laughing.

Two more days passed and she felt quite well

again. Even her cold had cleared up and Klaus, looking her over carefully each morning, had to admit at
last that he could find nothing wrong with her, a remark which caused her to ask: 'Well, when's Professor van der Blocq coming back?'

Klaus put down his coffee cup and looked at her
in bewilderment. 'Coming back? But he has never
been away.' His pleasant face cleared. 'Ah, you mean
when does he come back to his house? Very soon, I
should suppose, for I am able to give him a good
account of you today, so surely he will not allow you
to return to your home.' He grinned at her disarm-
ingly. 'He is not of our generation, the chief—he
holds old-fashioned views about things which we
younger men think nothing of.'

She went a bright, angry pink. 'Don't talk as
though he were an old man!' she said sharply. 'And
I share his views.'

Klaus smiled ruefully. 'I see that I must beg your
pardon, and I do so most sincerely. You must not
think that I mock at the chief—he is a mighty man
in surgery and a good man in his life and much liked
and respected—I myself would wish to be like him.'
He looked at her with curiosity. 'You knew, then, that
he was living in the hospital until you are well enough
to leave his house?'

'Of course.' Her voice, even to her own ears,
sounded satisfyingly convincing. 'I am his ward, you
know. It's like having a father…'

The absurdity of the remark struck her even as she
made it. Fabian was no more like a father than the

young man sitting opposite her. 'Well, not quite,' she conceded, 'but you know what I mean.'

He agreed politely, although she could see that he had little idea of what she meant; she wasn't certain herself. He got up to go presently, wishing her good-bye because he didn't expect to see her again, 'Although I daresay that you will visit your guardian from time to time,' he hazarded, 'and I expect to be here for some years.'

She gave him a smiling reply, longing for him to go so that she could have time to herself to think. To learn that Fabian had been in Groningen all the time she had been at his house, and had made no effort to come and see her, had been a shock she was just beginning to realize. Maybe he was old-fashioned in his views, she was herself, and she could respect him for them, but not even the most strait-laced member of the community could have seen any objection to him going to see her in his own house—or telephoning, for that matter—and surely he could have said something to her? There was only one possible explanation, he was quite indifferent to her; considered her a nuisance he felt obliged to suffer until she was fit to return home. It would have been nice to have confronted him with this, but then he might ask her how it was that she knew he had been in Groningen, and unless she could think of some brilliant lie, poor Klaus would get the blame for speaking out of turn. She allowed several possibilities, most of them highly impractical, to flit through her head before deciding regretfully that she was a poor liar in any case, and she would not have the nerve, not with Fabian's dark, penetrating gaze bent upon her, so she discarded them all to explore other possibilities.

She could run away—a phrase she hastily changed to beating a retreat—if she did that, it would save Fabian the necessity of arranging her journey and at the same time save her pride and allow him to see that she was quite able to look after herself. She didn't need his help, she told herself firmly, in future she would have nothing to do with him. Doubtless he would be delighted—had he not told her that she was tiresome to him? Mary Jane paced up and down the comfortable room, in a splendid rage which was almost, but not quite, strong enough to conceal her love for him. But for the time being, it served its purpose—she would write him a letter, thanking him for all he had done... She began to plot, sitting before the fire in the pleasant room.

By lunch-time she had it all worked out, she would leave that very afternoon. She wouldn't be able to take her case with her, but Klaus had said that she might go for a short walk if she had a mind to. He had told Mevrouw Hol this—it made it all very easy; she had her passport and plenty of money still, she could buy what she needed as she went, and this time she would fly—it would be quicker and she supposed that there would be several flights to London once she got to Schiphol. She ate her lunch on a wave of false excitement and over her coffee began the letter to Fabian.

Her pen was poised over the paper while she composed a few dignified sentences in her head when the door opened and he walked in. If he saw her startled jump and the guilty way she tried to hide her writing pad and pen, he said nothing.

'Young Vliet tells me you're quite recovered,' he began without preamble. 'I've arranged for you to travel home this evening.'

She gazed at him speechlessly, feeling dreadfully deflated after all her careful planning, and when she didn't speak, he went on, 'I expected you to express instant delight, instead of which you look flabbergasted and dreadfully guilty. What have you been doing?'

'Nothing—nothing at all.' Her voice came out in a protesting, earnest squeak. 'I'm surprised, that's all. I—I was—that is…' She remembered something. 'Did you have a nice time in Utrecht?'

'Yes. I see you're writing letters—leave them here and I'll see that they're posted.'

She was breathless. 'No—that is, they're not important—there's no need…' She tore the sheet across and crumpled it up very small and threw it on the fire. She had only got as far as 'Dear Fabian,' but she didn't want him to see even that. She sighed loudly without knowing it and said with a brightness born of relief, 'There, I can write all the letters I want to when I get home.'

Fabian had seated himself opposite her and was pouring himself the coffee which Mevrouw Hol had just brought in. 'Not to Mervyn, I hope?'

'Mervyn?' She stared at him, her mouth a little

open. She had forgotten about Mervyn because there wasn't anyone else in the world while Fabian was there. 'Oh, Mervyn,' she said at last, 'no, of course not. I don't know where he is.' She stared at the hands in her lap. 'I don't want to know, either.'

'The temptation to say "I told you so" is very great, but I won't do that.' He put down his cup. 'The train leaves here about six o'clock—do you need anything or wish to go anywhere before you leave?'

He wanted her out of the way. She got to her feet and said coldly, 'No, thank you—I'll go and put a few things together...'

'Five minutes' work,' he was gently mocking, 'but it's as good an excuse as any, I imagine.' He went to the door and opened it for her. 'I shall be in the study if you should want anything,' he told her.

She made no attempt to pack her case when she reached her room; he was right, five minutes was more than enough time in which to cast her few things in and slam the lid. She sat down in the little bucket chair by the window and stared down into the little courtyard, not seeing it at all. It was a very good thing that she was going away, although perhaps not quite as she had planned. She should never have come in the first place, only Fabian had been so insistent. She allowed her thoughts to dwell briefly on Cousin Emma and Doctor Trouw and wondered if she would ever see them again—perhaps they would come and stay with her later on, then she would get news of Fabian. Although wasn't a clean break better? He had told her that her affairs were now in good order, anything which needed seeing to could be done by letter or through Mr North.

She got up and prowled round the room, touching its small treasures with a gentle finger—glass and porcelain and silver—Fabian had a lovely home and she would never forget it. Presently she sat down again and dozed off.

Mevrouw Hol wakened her for tea, bustling into the room, wanting to know if she felt well and was she cold, or would she like her tea in her room. Mary Jane shook her head to each question and went downstairs. There was no sign of Fabian; she ate her tea as she had always done, from a tray on the small table by the fire. He must have gone back to the hospital. She poured a second cup, wondering if he had left instructions as to how she was to get to the station.

She finished her tea and went back upstairs to ram her things into her case in a most untidy, uncaring fashion, not in the least like her usual neat ways, and, that done, went back downstairs and out to the kitchen where Mevrouw Hol was preparing dinner. Mary Jane watched her for a moment and asked in her frightful Dutch: 'People for dinner?' and when Mevrouw Hol nodded, felt a pang of pure envy and curiosity shoot through her. 'How many?' she wanted to know.

The housekeeper shot her a thoughtful glance. 'Three,' she said, 'two ladies and a gentleman.'

'Married?' asked Mary Jane before she could stop herself.

Mevrouw Hol nodded, and Mary Jane, her imagination at work again, had a vivid mental picture of

some distinguished couple, and—the crux of the
whole matter—a beautiful girl—blonde, and wearing
couture clothes, she decided, her imagination working
overtime. She would have a disdainful look and Fabian would adore her. She got down from the edge
of the table where she had perched herself. 'I'll get
ready,' she said in her terrible Dutch.

She went downstairs at twenty to six, because Fabian had said that the train went at six o'clock, and
perhaps she should get a taxi. She was hatted and
coated and ready to leave and there was no sign of
anyone. Fabian came out of his study as she reached
the hall. He said briefly: 'I'll get your case,' and when
he came downstairs again she ventured, 'Should I call
a taxi—there's not much time.' She searched his tranquil face. 'I didn't know you'd come back,' she explained.

'I've been here all the afternoon—I had some work
to do. If you're ready we'll go.'

'Oh—are you taking me to the station? I
thought...'

'Never mind what you thought. Don't you agree
that as your guardian the least I can do is to see you
safely on the way to England?'

She had no answer to that but went in search of
Mevrouw Hol, who shook her by the hand and wished
her *'Tot ziens,'* adding a great deal in her own language which Mary Jane couldn't understand in the
least.

The journey to the station was short, a matter of a
few minutes, during which Mary Jane sought vainly

for something to say. She couldn't believe that she was actually going—that perhaps she might not see Fabian again for a long time, perhaps never, for he had no reason to see her again.

She looked sideways at his calm profile and then at his gloved hands resting on the wheel. She loved him very much; she had no idea that loving someone could hurt so fiercely. She went with him silently into the station and on to the platform and found the train already there. She watched while Fabian spoke to the guard, took the tickets which he handed to her and thanked him in a small voice.

'There's a seat in the dining car reserved for you,' he told her. 'Someone will fetch you. The guard will see about a porter for you when you reach the Hoek. Just go on board, everything is arranged. There's a seat booked on the breakfast car from Harwich. Have you your headache tablets with you?'

'Yes, thank you, and thank you for taking so much trouble, Fabian.'

'You had better get in,' he advised her, and disappeared, to reappear within a few minutes with a bundle of magazines. 'Don't read too much,' he told her.

She lingered on the steps. 'I must owe you quite a bit—for the journey—shall I send it to you?'

'Don't bother. Mr North will settle with me.' He put out a hand. 'Goodbye, Mary Jane, have a good trip.'

She shook hands and answered him in a steady voice—how useful pride could be on occasion! She even added a few meaningless phrases, the sort of thing one says when one is bidding someone goodbye at a railway station. He dismissed them with a half smile and got out of the train. She watched him getting smaller and smaller as the train gathered speed and finally went round a curve, and then he was gone.

The journey was smooth and so well organised that she had no worries at all; it was as though an unseen Fabian was there, smoothing her path. She wondered to what trouble he had gone to have made everything so easy for her. It was a pity that his thoughtfulness was partly wasted, for she spent a wretched night and no amount of make-up could help the pallor of her face or the tell-tale puffiness of her eyelids. She arrived, thoroughly dispirited, at Liverpool Street station in the cold rain of the January morning, and the first person she saw was Mrs Body.

CHAPTER NINE

LATER, LOOKING BACK on that morning, Mary Jane knew that she had reached the end of her tether by the time she had reached London, although she hadn't known it then, only felt an upsurge of relief and delight at the sight of Mrs Body in her sensible tweeds and best hat. She had almost fallen out of the train in her eagerness to get to her and fling herself at the older woman, and Mrs Body, standing four-square amidst the hurrying passengers, had given her a motherly hug and sensibly made no remark about her miserable face, but had said merely that the dear doctor had been quite right to ask her to come to London, much though she disliked the place, for by all accounts Mary Jane had had a nasty bang on the head. She then hurried her into a taxi and on to the next train for home, and Mary Jane, exhausted by her feelings more than the rigours of the journey, slept most of the way.

She had been home for almost a week now, a week during which she had filled her days with chores around the house and long walks with a delighted Major trailing at her heels. Her evenings she spent chatting with Mrs Body, talking about the village and what had happened in it while she had been away, various household matters, and the state of the garden.

Of Holland she spoke not at all, excepting to touch lightly upon the wedding and her fall, and to her relief neither Mrs Body nor Lily had displayed any curiosity as to what she had done while she was there, nor, after that one remark Mrs Body had made on Liverpool Street station, had Fabian been mentioned. It should have made it all the easier to erase him from her mind, but it did no such thing; she found herself thinking of him constantly, his face, with its remote expression and the little smile which so disconcerted her, floated before her eyes last thing at night, and was there waiting for her when she wakened in the morning; it was really very vexing.

She tried inviting a few of her grandfather's old friends in for drinks one evening and realised too late that they were deeply interested in her visits to Holland, and wanted to know all about that country, and what was more, about her guardian too. They discussed him at some length—very much to his advantage, she was quick to note—and old Mr North, when asked to add his opinion to those of the other elderly gentlemen present, observed that, in his judgement, Jonkheer van der Blocq was a man of integrity, very much to be trusted and the right man to solve any problem. 'That episode with Mr Mervyn Pettigrew, for example,' he began, and then coughed dryly. 'I beg your pardon, Mary Jane, I should not have mentioned him; doubtless your feelings on the matter are still painful.'

He smiled kindly at her, as did his companions, and she smiled gently back, happily conscious that her feelings weren't painful at all, at least not about Mervyn. 'It doesn't matter,' she assured them, 'I got over that some time ago.' She realised as she said it that it was only a few weeks since her heart had been broken and had mended itself so quickly. 'I made a mistake,' she said calmly. 'Luckily it was discovered in time.'

'Indeed yes, and solely due to your guardian's efforts. To travel to Canada when everyone was enjoying their Christmas showed great determination on his part. I feel that your future is in safe hands, my dear.'

The other gentlemen murmured agreement, and Mary Jane, busy playing hostess, wished with all her heart that what Mr North had said was true; there was nothing she would have liked better than to have had a safe future with Fabian, not quite such a one as her companions envisaged perhaps, but infinitely more interesting.

The next morning, urged on by a desire to do something, no matter what, she took the Mini to Carlisle and bought clothes. She really didn't need them; she had plenty of sensible tweeds and jersey dresses and several evening outfits which, as far as she could see, she couldn't hope to wear out, let alone wear. She had bought them when Mervyn had come to visit her. Now, speeding towards the shops, she decided that she loathed the sight of them; she would give them all away and buy something new.

Once having made this resolve, she found that nothing could stop her; several dresses she bought for the very good reason that they were pretty and she

looked nice in them, even though she could think of
no occasion when she might wear them. She balanced
this foolishness by purchasing a couple of outfits
which she could wear each day, and, her conscience
salved, bought several pairs of shoes, expensive ones,
quite unsuitable for the life she led, and undies, all
colours of the rainbow.

She bought a red dressing gown for Mrs Body too,
and more glamorous undies for Lily, who was going
steady with the postman and was making vague plans
for a wedding in the distant future.

She and Mrs Body and Lily spent an absorbing
evening, inspecting her purchases, but later, when she
was alone in her room, she hung the gay dresses
away, wondering wistfully if she would ever wear
them. It seemed unlikely, but it wasn't much good
brooding over it. She closed the closet door upon
them and got into bed, where she lay, composing a
letter to Fabian, reminding him that she still hadn't
got a horse to ride. The exercise kept her mind occupied for some time and although she knew that she
would never write it, and certainly not send it, it gave
her a kind of satisfaction. She should have said something about it in the short, stiff letter she had written
to him when she arrived home, a conventional enough
missive, thanking him for his thoughtful arrangement
of her journey and his care of her while she had been
in hospital. It had taken her a long time to write and
she had wasted several sheets of notepaper before the
composition had satisfied her. He hadn't answered it.

The weather, which had been almost springlike for

a few days, worsened the next morning, with cold grey clouds covering the sky, a harsh wind whistling through the bare trees and a light powdering of snow covering the ground. A beastly day, thought Mary Jane, looking out of the window while she pulled on her slacks and two sweaters. She had promised Mrs Body and Lily most of the day off too, to attend a wedding in the village, and heaven knew what time they would get back; weddings were something of an event in their quiet community and the occasion of lengthy hospitality. With an eye to the worsening weather, Mary Jane saw them off after an early lunch and went back to the kitchen to wash up and set the tea tray. This done, she wandered into the sitting room. It looked inviting with a bright fire burning and Major snoozing before it, but there was a lot of the day to get through still; she decided on a walk, a long one down to the lake and along its shore for a few miles and then back over the hills, and if the weather got too bad she could always take to the road. It would get rid of the restlessness she felt, she told herself firmly, and went to put on an old mackintosh and gumboots.

They set off, she and Major, ten minutes later—it was no day for a walk, but she was content to plod along in the teeth of the wind, thinking about Fabian, and Major was content to plod with her.

They got back home at the end of a prematurely darkened afternoon—the snow had settled a little, despite the wind, and the daylight had almost gone. The cold had become pitiless. Mary Jane and Major, tired and longing for tea and the fire, turned in at the gate and hurried up the short drive. The house looked as cold as its surroundings; she wished she had left a lamp burning as a welcome, then she remembered as she reached the door that she hadn't locked it behind her—not that that mattered, she had Major with her. But Major had other ideas; he had left her to go round the side of the house to the back door; years of training having fixed in his doggy mind that on wet days he had to go in through the garden porch.

She went in alone, pulling off her outdoor things as she went and casting them down anyhow. The hall was almost in darkness and she shivered, not from cold but because she was lonely and unhappy. She said quite loudly in a miserable voice: 'Oh, Fabian!' and came to a sudden shocked halt when he said from the dimness, 'Hullo, Mary Jane.'

She turned to stare at him dimly outlined against the sitting room door and heard his voice, very matter-of-fact, again. 'You left the door open.'

She nodded into the gloom, temporarily speechless, but presently she managed, 'Have you come about my horse?'

'No.'

She waited, but that seemed to be all that he was going to say, and suddenly unable to bear it any longer, she said in a voice a little too loud: 'Please will you go?'

'If you will give me a good reason—yes.'

She didn't feel quite herself. She supposed it was

the shock of finding him there, but she seemed to have lost all control over her tongue.

'I've been very silly,' her voice was still too loud, but she didn't care. 'It's you I love. I think I've always loved you, but I didn't know—Mervyn was you, if you see what I mean.' She added, quite distraught: 'So please will you go away—now.' Her voice shook a little, her mouth felt dry. She urged: 'Please, Fabian.'

He made no movement. 'What a girl you are for missing the obvious,' he observed pleasantly. 'Why do you suppose I've come?'

She wasn't really listening, being completely taken up with the appalling realisation of her foolish and impetuous speech, but she supposed he expected an answer so she said, 'Oh, the horse—no, you said it wasn't, didn't you. Have I spent too much money? You could have written about that, there was no need for you to have come...'

He crossed the hall and took her in his arms. 'You're a silly girl,' he told her, and his voice was very tender. 'Of course there is a need. Only perhaps I have been silly too—you see, my darling, you are so young and I—I am forty.'

'Oh, what has that got to do with it?' she demanded quite crossly. 'You could be twenty or ninety; you'd still be Fabian, can't you see that?'

His arms tightened around her. 'I'll remember that,' he told her softly, 'my adorable Miss Pettigrew,' and when she would have spoken he drew her a little closer. 'Hush, my love—my darling love. I'm not sure when I fell in love with you, perhaps when we first met, although I wasn't aware of it—that came later, the night Uncle Georgius died and I opened the sitting-room door and you were on the stairs looking lost and unhappy. But after that you were never there, always disappearing when I came. I waited and waited, hoping that you would love me too, and then Mervyn turned up. I have never been so worried...'

'You didn't look worried,' Mary Jane pointed out.

'Perhaps I'm not very good at showing my feelings,' he told her, 'but I'll try now.' She was wrapped in his arms as though he would never let her go again—a state, she thought dreamily, to which she was happily resigned, and when he kissed her she had no more thoughts at all. Presently she said into his shoulder, 'I was going to run away, but you came back. I thought you didn't like me being in your house—that you wanted me to come back here.'

He loosed his hold a little so that he could see her face. 'My dearest darling, there was nothing I wanted more than to have you in my home, but you were my ward...'

'You let me go.' She frowned a little, staring up into his dark eyes. 'You arranged for me to go.'

'Because I knew that you would run away if I didn't—you see, my love, I know you better than you know yourself.' He pulled her quite roughly to him and kissed her thoroughly. 'I haven't been the best of guardians, but I shall be a very good husband,' he promised her, and kissed her again, very gently this time.

It was quite dark in the hall by now, and Major, fed up with waiting at the back door, pattered in and came to sit down beside them, thumping his tail on the floor. 'He wants his supper,' said Mary Jane in a dreamy voice.

'So do I, my darling girl.'

She wasn't dreamy any more. 'Oh, my darling Fabian, you're hungry! I'll cook something.' But when she would have slipped from his arms he held her fast. 'Not just yet...'

'We can't stay here all night—Mrs Body and Lily won't be back for ages—they've gone to a wedding.' She smiled up at him, quite content to stay where she was for ever.

'They shall come to ours, my darling.'

'Oh, Fabian!' She could hardly see his face although it was so close to her own, but that didn't matter, nothing mattered any more. Life had become blissfully perfect, stretching out before them for ever. She clasped her hands behind his neck and because she couldn't put her happiness into words, she said again, 'Oh, Fabian!' and kissed him.

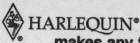

Uncover the truth behind

CODE NAME: DANGER

in **Merline Lovelace's** thrilling duo

DANGEROUS TO HOLD

When tricky situations need a cool head, quick wits and a touch
of ruthlessness, Adam Ridgeway, director of the top secret
OMEGA agency, sends in his team. Lately, though, his agents have
had romantic troubles of their own....

NIGHT OF THE JAGUAR
&
THE COWBOY AND THE COSSACK

And don't miss
HOT AS ICE (IM #1129, 2/02)
which features the newest OMEGA adventure!

DANGEROUS TO HOLD is available this February
at your local retail outlet!

Look for ***DANGEROUS TO KNOW,*** the second set of
stories in this collection, in July 2002.

Silhouette®

Where love comes alive™

Visit Silhouette at www.eHarlequin.com   PSDTH